A CRIME OF PASSION

A CRIME OF PASSION

By

SCOTT PRATT

ISBN: 0692312374
ISBN 13: 9780692312377

This book, along with every book I've written and every book I'll write, is dedicated to my darling Kristy, to her unconquerable spirit and her inspirational courage. I loved her before I was born and I'll love her after I'm long gone.

"You are the exclusive judges of the facts in this case. Also, you are the exclusive judges of the law under the direction of the court. You should apply the law to the facts in deciding this case. You should consider all of the evidence in the light of your own observations and experience in life."

Tennessee Criminal Pattern Jury Instructions – Section 1.08

"Statements, arguments, and remarks of counsel are intended to help you in understanding the evidence and applying the law, but they are not evidence. If any statements were made that you believe are not supported by the evidence, you should disregard them."

Tennessee Criminal Pattern Jury Instructions – Section 1.07

PROLOGUE

The redhead stared across the desk at the lawyer, her blue eyes smoldering. She had requested an after-hours meeting so everyone would be gone. It hadn't quite worked out that way—high-priced, big-city lawyers worked late—but there were only a couple people left in the sprawling, twenty-fifth floor office suite that over-looked the Cumberland River and downtown Nashville.

"How much have I paid you over the years, Carl?" she said in an edgy voice.

The lawyer shrugged and held her gaze. "Not enough for me to get involved in a murder conspiracy."

"Nobody is asking you to get involved," she said. "All I want is a contact. A point of entry. A name. The name of a company. Just get me something. I'll take care of the rest."

"I should probably make you aware at this point that the attorney-client privilege does not extend to situations in which the client attempts to involve the attorney in a crime."

"Damn it, Carl, have you gone deaf? I just said you don't have to get involved. Do you know what would happen if I went out on the street with something like this?

I'd wind up hiring some inept thug for $15,000. Or worse, I'd hire a cop and find myself in jail."

"Then don't do it," said Carl Browning, a fifty-year-old, balding, bespectacled senior partner at Allen, Parks, Browning and Cummings. Browning had represented Lana Raines-Milius, the redheaded former country music diva, for eight years. Lana was devious and could be difficult, but she was mega-rich, and there were also some occasional benefits that Browning found unspeakably delicious.

"I have to do it," Lana said.

"Why?"

"He *deserves* it. All the things he's done in the past? And now he's screwing a child."

"Are you sure about that?"

"I know what I know."

"Why don't you just divorce him?"

"Because it would take years and the only people who would benefit would be people like you."

"I don't handle divorce cases, Lana."

"I can't believe this hasn't come up before," Lana said. "In all the years you've practiced law, all the rich, high-powered clients you've worked with, you can't tell me that you've never had anyone approach you with something like this."

"I didn't say that," Browning said. "What I said was I'm not going to involve myself in a murder conspiracy."

"So it's come up," Lana said, with just a hint of a smile beginning to cross her lips.

"Maybe. Once or twice."

"And you know where to go."

"I might."

"I love it when you play the hard-to-get game," Lana said. She stood and walked to the office door, locked it, and turned back toward Browning. She walked slowly around his desk, unbuttoning her blouse as she moved. She stopped a couple feet from him, slipped out of the blouse, and laid it on the desk. The lawyer rolled his high-backed chair away from the desk and turned to face her. She took a step closer and kneeled.

"You know what kind of resources I have," Lana said softly as she reached for his belt buckle. "But I also want you to know that I'm willing to do whatever it takes to get this done and get it done right. Quick and clean. I already have the room number of the hotel where I want it done. I have the date. I've done my homework. Nobody will ever know a thing—except for you and me."

"And the contractor," Browning said.

Lana slowly unzipped the lawyer's fly and licked her lips seductively.

"Shall we begin to conspire?" she said as her mouth opened and she leaned in toward him. "Just one little contact. One little name."

PART I

CHAPTER 1

Alex Pappas heard his office door open, looked up, and his heart went cold. Lana Milius was walking in. Alex's boss's wife. The burned-out diva. The spoiled-rotten-woman-child who would slash the throat of a baby seal if she wanted to wear a sealskin coat. No, no. Lana wouldn't slash the throat herself. She'd find a way to get someone else to do it for her. But she'd wear the coat.

Alex had been working for Paul Milius for three years, and were it not for Lana, his would be a dream job. Being the personal assistant to Paul Milius, the owner of the biggest and most powerful record company in Nashville, was demanding but interesting. He made great money, and he lived in an incredible house on a spectacular estate. He liked Paul okay—with the exception that he was aloof and distant—but he liked Paul's life better. It was busy and filled with all sorts of fascinating people, everything from artsy troubadours to cutthroat businessmen. But he didn't think much of Paul's choice of a wife. Lana had been a big shot before Alex came onto the scene, a platinum-coated country music artist. She was still pretty, even beautiful, but whenever Alex saw her, only one word came to mind, a word that started with "b" and rhymed with rich.

"Hidy, Allie," Lana said in her best hick voice. She was wearing her standard around-the-house attire—a silk kimono, this one all purple and floral and cut low around her chest and high around her thighs. On her feet were black, open-toed sandals with four-inch heels, and across her shoulders was a sheer, pink scarf. She looked like a French hooker playing geisha girl. This was an "I want something from you" outfit. Alex had seen it several times before. He forced himself to smile.

"Hello, Mrs. Milius."

"Why do you always have to be so formal with me, Allie? Don't you like me?"

She tossed the name "Allie" at him like a dart, and each time she did, it penetrated just a bit deeper beneath his skin.

"I like you just fine, Mrs. Milius."

Alex watched uncomfortably as Lana walked behind him. She dropped one end of her scarf on his right shoulder and pulled it across his back as she continued to walk around his desk.

"I need a little favor from you, Allie," Lana said.

"What kind of favor?"

"Just a couple minor things. I need you to provide some information to some people using an encrypted email, maybe transfer some money to them."

"An encrypted email? Sounds clandestine."

"Ooh, I like that word. *Clandestine.* Yes, it's all very clandestine," Lana said as she sat down in a chair across from Alex's desk and crossed her legs. "Very hush, hush.

Big business, you know? I need someone who knows their way around modern communications technology."

"I don't know, Mrs. Milius. I think I'd have to have a little more information—"

"Are you refusing a request from your employer?" Lana snapped.

"Paul is my employer," Alex said.

"*We* are your employer," Lana said. "A corporation employs you and all the rest of the people who work here. And guess who the president and chief executive officer of the corporation that owns all our properties happens to be? Little ol' me. I'll bet you never thought about that, did you? Not that you *should* be thinking about things like that. As a matter of fact, right now, what you should be thinking about the most is how to please Lana Raines-Milius. You should be asking yourself exactly what she wants and exactly what you're going to do to make sure she gets what she wants."

Alex held up his hand, almost defensively. "Hold on, Mrs. Milius. You're not making any sense. Exactly why are you here?"

"See? There you go, right there," Lana said. "Now you've got it. I'm here because I need you to do *exactly* what I tell you for the next few days without saying a word to anyone. I'm going to provide you with some computer files and a prepaid cell phone, and I'm going to give you access to some money. You're going to set up an email account and send the files to the people I tell you to send them to. You're going to talk to them on the telephone if it becomes necessary, and you're going to transfer money when and where I tell you."

Alex's eyes narrowed as he listened. He'd always suspected Lana was capable of some unseemly things, but he hadn't expected her to involve him.

"And if I refuse?" Alex said.

"Let's not even talk about that," Lana said as she uncrossed her legs, revealing that she wasn't wearing panties. She re-crossed them quickly as Alex's mind flashed to an old movie he'd seen. What was it called? *Basic Instinct.* "Let's talk about what's in it for you if you do what I ask you to do. First of all, there's this." The legs uncrossed again, and Lana kept them that way for ten seconds while she stared directly into Alex's eyes. "Any time you want it. Oh, and there are these." She reached up slowly and pulled the kimono down to reveal her breasts.

"Mrs. Milius, please," Alex said. "No offense, but I'm not interested in having sex with you. It just wouldn't be…it wouldn't be right."

"Well listen to you, the perfect little gentleman," Lana said as she pulled the kimono back up and crossed her legs. "You've been having sex with Tilly, haven't you?"

"I beg your pardon?"

"Don't play games with me, Allie. I know everything that goes on inside this house and half of what goes on outside. You and Tilly have been seeing each other for six months. Don't tell me you haven't sampled the goods."

"My relationship with Tilly is none of your business."

"You're so cute when you're angry," Lana said. "Your cute little lips tighten up in a line, and your pretty little jaw starts to twitch."

"I'd appreciate it if you'd leave now," Alex said.

"But I'm not finished. I haven't told you what else is in it for you if you do what I ask. I'll give you a half million in cash if everything goes the way I want it to."

"Then it can't be legal," Alex said. "You're asking me to do something illegal."

Lana held the scarf in front of her face and started waving it back and forth. "*Legality*," she said. "*Morality*. They're just words. Who's to say what's legal and what isn't? Who's to say what's moral and what isn't? I don't feel bound by any of that. I do what I think is best for me."

"Why don't you just do whatever it is you want done yourself?" Alex said.

"Because I don't want to take a chance on getting caught. It would be awful if I was caught. I could go to jail."

"But it's all right if I go to jail?"

"Better you than me," Lana said. Her tone suddenly turned from syrupy to icy. "I've tried to be nice, Allie, but you're making it impossible, so let me just tell you what will happen if you *don't* do what I want. You can forget the half-million dollars. That offer is rescinded. May I borrow a pen and a piece of paper? Please, just a sticky note will be fine. That's it."

Lana rose from her chair while Alex slid an ink pen and a pad of blue sticky notes across the desk. She leaned over and wrote something on the top sticky note, pulled it off, and set it down in front of Alex. Then she did it again. And again. Lana straightened up and smiled while Alex gazed down at the three small pieces of paper. On each one of them was what looked to be a perfect forgery of his signature.

"You know that black Centurion credit card that Paul lets you use? Well, you've been using it an awful lot lately. Do you know where it is, by the way?"

Alex reached into his pocket and pulled out a set of keys. He opened a desk drawer to his right, took out a small, leather case. It was empty. He began to feel nauseous.

"Oh, my," Lana said. "It's gone, isn't it? Do you know you've run up more than $200,000 in unauthorized credit card purchases in the past two weeks? You've bought some beautiful jewelry for Tilly, which the police will find if they happen to get involved. You've also bought some extremely nice things for yourself, things that will find their way into your closet when the police come. I called one of my lawyers and asked him what would happen to someone who had stolen $200,000 from his employer, and he said that person would go to prison for at least eight years. And I'm sure you're aware that Paul knows most of the judges in town. If he thought you'd stolen all that money from him, I'm sure he'd make sure you went straight to jail. You wouldn't pass go. You wouldn't collect $200. You'd just go straight to jail for a long, long time."

Alex was so stunned he could think of nothing to say. He just looked at Lana, open-mouthed.

"And just in case you're still not convinced," Lana said, "I'm sure the people we're dealing with would treat Tilly very harshly if you were to try anything silly, like telling Paul or going to the police."

"She's your cousin, for God's sake," Alex said. "She's been nothing but good to you."

"So you'll come over to our wing and meet me in my office then," Lana said. "Let's say about thirty minutes? I have something I need to give you, and then maybe we'll have a little fun."

CHAPTER 2

The lawyer eased his Jaguar onto I-65 north and looked at Lana Raines-Milius.

"All the arrangements have been finalized," Carl Browning said. "Is Alex on board?"

"He's on board," Lana said. "He's not happy about it, but I gave him the cell phone. How much is this going to cost?"

"Five million. Half on the front end and half when it's done."

"Five million? Five million! Are you serious?"

"That doesn't include my fee," Browning said. "Listen, you wanted this done right. You want to have it happen when and where you want it to happen and you want it clean. It can be done. It's been done before, many times, and it's been done in such a way that nobody knew what really happened. That's what you want, am I correct?"

"That's what I want, but five million?"

"These people are consummate professionals. There are maybe three organizations in the entire world that do what they do, and only one that operates within the United States. Nobody does it better. We could find individuals, freelancers, who would do it cheaper, but there are so many risks if we go that route that I wouldn't even consider it. This is the way to go, Lana. It's expensive, but if you look at the rewards in comparison with the risk… well, you stand to gain a great deal."

Lana nodded. "I know. Nothing has changed with Paul's will?"

"I think he'd like to change it, but at this point, he hasn't. You know how it is with people's wills. They don't want to think about it."

"So I'm the sole beneficiary?"

"You'll come out of this smelling like the proverbial rose."

"How much are you going to charge me?"

"Ten percent of the contract price, so add another $500,000. Plus benefits."

"You're a real peach, Carl."

"Nothing will ever be traced back to you. It's a bargain."

"Where's the money coming from?" Lana asked.

"I'll channel it through your foundation."

Lana laughed out loud. "Does that mean it'll get written off on a tax return?"

"It does. A beautiful irony, isn't it?"

CHAPTER 3

My name is Joe Dillard, and the call that led me to the world of Paul and Lana Milius came on Christmas Eve. The family had gathered. My son, Jack, and his girlfriend, Charleston "Charlie" Story, were home from Nashville for the holidays and were staying with my wife, Caroline, and me. My daughter, Lilly, her husband, Randy, and their son, Joseph, were also at the house, along with my sister, Sarah, and her daughter, Grace. We were doing what people do at Christmas. We'd eaten a nice dinner that Caroline and I had cooked, we'd exchanged gifts, and we were sitting around drinking wine, listening to Christmas music, laughing and playing with the kids when my cell rang. I wouldn't have answered it had I not seen "Leon Bates" on the screen. Leon had been the sheriff of Washington County, Tennessee, for a long time, and as far as I could tell, he would remain the sheriff for as long as he wanted. He was a rare breed, an excellent lawman, an even better politician, and a decent human being. He and I were close friends, but he didn't routinely call me on Christmas Eve.

"Merry Christmas, Sheriff," I said.

"Merry Christmas to you, Brother Dillard," Leon said in his smooth drawl.

"What's Santa going to bring you this year?"

"Ah, probably a bag of hair or a box of rocks. Maybe both. I ain't been a very good boy."

"I find that hard to believe," I said. "You're a pillar of the community, Leon. A seeker of justice, a towering hunk of righteous, manly man—"

"You been drinkin' a little there, Brother Dillard?"

"Yeah, I'm working on my third glass of wine, so I'm about half in the bag. What's up, Leon? What has caused you to reach out to me on this very special holiday evening?"

"I called to see if you'd be interested in getting rich."

"Rich? As in wealthy rich?"

"As in a million dollars rich."

I got up and walked out the door onto the back deck. The air was cold and crisp, the sky clear and full of brilliant stars.

"If you're serious, Leon, you have my undivided attention."

"Never been more serious in my life. Did you hear about that little ol' gal—country singer—that turned up dead in a hotel room in Nashville a couple weeks ago? It was all over the news."

"Yeah, yeah. Kasey something...Cartwright? Kasey Cartwright. She was from Boones Creek or Gray, wasn't she?"

"That's her. Pretty thing, voice like a nightingale. Wrote good songs, too. I saw her in concert when I was in Nashville back in September. One of the best guitar pickers I've ever seen. Played the banjo, the fiddle, and the piano, too. Her dying at such a young age was a damned shame."

"Seems like I heard something about an overdose. I thought they ruled her death an accident or maybe a suicide."

"There wasn't any overdose. That was just gossip reporters being gossip reporters, making stuff up. They ruled it a homicide after they did an autopsy and found out her hyoid bone had been crushed. Surprised you didn't hear that. There's been a lot of speculation about who did it, but turns out they made an arrest earlier today."

"Who got arrested?"

"Man by the name of Paul Milius. Ever heard of him?"

"Can't say that I have."

"Owns a company called Perseus Records, the record company that pretty much owned Kasey Cartwright, at least the professional part of her anyway. Nice enough man. I talked to him a few times at political get-togethers in Nashville, and we wound up hitting it off so well that he invited me down to his house in Franklin a couple times. Paul discovered Kasey Cartwright back when she was fifteen is the way the story goes. Signed her to a record deal and started building her career. Turned her into a big star. Would have turned her into a superstar if she'd lived."

"Which means he turned her into a cash cow. Why would he kill his cash cow?"

I heard Leon's signature chuckle. It was throaty, both pleasant and infectious.

"That's why I like you so much, Brother Dillard," he said after a few seconds. "There you are, sitting at the house on the night before Christmas, half in the bag—as you put it—and I lay out a little scenario for you and you cut right to the chase. Why *would* he kill his cash cow? That's a question that's being asked all over Nashville as we speak. And I mean *all over* Nashville. Paul Milius is worth hundreds of millions of dollars, and hundreds of millions of dollars will buy you a lot of powerful friends in the capitol city of the great state of Tennessee. Those powerful friends are all wondering the same thing, and apparently Paul Milius is screaming to high heaven that he didn't do it."

"Speaking of cutting to the chase, what does this have to do with me?"

"Milius's wife wants you to help defend him," Leon said.

"Why? She's never heard of me."

"Okay, I'll give you that. You're probably right. I doubt that she'd ever heard of you until recently. But some friends of hers have heard of you, and they want you to defend him."

"What friends?"

"Me, most importantly. I've been making friends in high places in Nashville for years and years, and like I said a minute ago, Paul and Lana Milius are among those friends. Paul is in jail right now. I just got off the phone with his wife, Lana. She says he's in shock, which is understandable, especially if he's really innocent. She wants him to have the best lawyer they can get. I know you think of yourself as a ham-and-egger, but you've built quite a reputation. Getting yourself appointed district attorney after Mooney tried to kill you, then all that with John Lipscomb and those boys from Colombia, then rescuing the little girl that was kidnapped—"

"Don't remind me of all that bad stuff, Leon. It's Christmas." I was a touch wounded that he'd called me a "ham-and-egger." I didn't think of myself as a high-pow-ered game changer, but I thought I was maybe a touch above a ham-and-egger.

"I was right there with you in the middle of all of it, and I don't regret a thing," Leon said. "But we're getting off track here. I've told Lana all about you, and she wants to hire you. They've had their company lawyers advising Paul up to this point—which wasn't none too bright, if you ask me—and I think the advice was bad. Paul's talked to the police a couple times, and he voluntarily gave them a DNA sample."

"That's not good, Leon. Do the cops have a DNA match?"

"My contacts at the Nashville PD say they do. A small piece of skin that was wedged between the victim's teeth. Turns out that skin belonged to Paul, but he still swears he didn't kill the girl. His wife believes him. Hell, *I* believe him. Lana wants you to go down there, run the case, and then handle the trial if it gets that far. I told them you wouldn't do it for less than a million retainer, nonrefund-able, plus expenses. Paul Milius can pay that out of the cookie jar on top of his refrigerator. He can also afford to post whatever bond you can talk a judge into setting."

"My wife has cancer, Leon. I can't go to Nashville."

"I thought she was doing well."

"She is, but that doesn't mean I'm going to run off three hundred miles away and do a murder case that could take a year or more."

"Demand a speedy trial. Get the judge to try him quick. And you can negotiate with Paul. He has a private jet. I've been on it. Make him fly you down there and back whenever you want. You can get Nashville lawyers to do the legwork for you. Hell, Brother Dillard, you're a good negotiator. You can get whatever you want out of Paul."

"You really told them a million?"

"I swear on the memory of my sweet momma."

"And you think they'll pay it?"

"I wouldn't be talking to you if I didn't."

"You know, the biggest fee I ever got from a client was $250,000 from Erlene Barlowe back before you became sheriff. This would make that look like peanuts."

"Erlene told me how much she paid you, plus she said she paid you another good lick to get *her* out of trouble. She doesn't begrudge a dime of it."

"You still seeing her?"

"She's in the kitchen making banana pudding. You want to holler at her?"

"Another time, Leon. Tell her I said, 'Merry Christmas.' Let me sleep on this."

"I told 'em you'd want to think about it a day or two, but don't take too long. They're a pretty itchy bunch."

"I'll let you know something within forty-eight hours."

"Sounds good. Merry Christmas, Brother Dillard. I hope Santy Claus brings you a bushel and a peck of everything you want. Plus a million smackeroos."

CHAPTER 4

When I went back into the living room, everyone was watching Sarah's three-year-old daughter, Grace, as she gave an impromptu performance of "The Dance of the Sugar Plum Fairy" in front of the Christmas tree. Caroline was sitting on the couch with her long legs crossed. She was wearing a red Christmas sweater and a white skirt. Her long, auburn hair was shining, and her brown eyes were glistening as the candles on the tables flickered. She had a glass of white wine in her right hand and a look of contentment on her face.

As I stood there looking at Caroline, I was reminded of how lucky I was to have her and how fortunate all of us were that she was still among us. Her battle with metastatic breast cancer had turned into a trench war with Caroline dug in on one end of the field and the disease dug in at the other. Caroline and her doctors lobbed medications like Fasolodex, Femara, Zoladex, and Zometa at the enemy, while the cancer simply dug in deeper and waited for a sign of weakness, anything that would allow it to strike or to mutate. It was a difficult and uncertain existence for all of us.

She had made it more than a year since the terrible diagnosis had been delivered that her cancer had metastasized to her bones. She'd fought through a terribly difficult round of radiation, through pain, nausea, fatigue, dry mouth, weight loss. She was doing well under the circumstances, but fear was always there, lurking like a monster under the bed. When would the cancer break out again and spread to her liver, her kidneys, her heart? Would the doctors be able to control it again? And always the ultimate question: how long did she have? The statistics gave her another year. Her doctor at Vanderbilt said she could live much longer, but none of us knew. We'd tried to "live like she was dying," as the Tim McGraw song says, to enjoy each day, each moment, to its fullest, but we'd found it impractical. We'd discovered that living the way we had always lived worked best for us, and we wanted it to last as long as possible.

"Who was that?" Caroline said to me after the dance was finished and the applause died down.

"Leon Bates."

"Leon? On Christmas Eve? What did he want?"

It probably wasn't the most appropriate time to discuss it, but I knew that eventually everyone in the family would weigh in on the subject. Since Leon wanted a decision quickly, and since the family was gathered and the mood was light, I decided to forge ahead.

"He wants me to take a murder case in Nashville. The retainer is a million dollars."

The news brought a collective gasp and a thirty-second silence.

"Is it Paul Milius?" Jack said. He was sitting on an overstuffed chair next to the couch with Charlie curled up on his lap.

"How did you know?"

"Ever heard of Facebook? Twitter? They're forms of social media that have been around for quite some time now. They're sometimes used to spread news very quickly."

"Wise ass," I said. I looked around at the rest of the group. "Yes, Paul Milius. Owns a record company in Nashville. He's accused of murdering an eighteen-year-old country singer named Kasey Cartwright two weeks ago."

"The girl from here?" Caroline asked.

"Yes. They apparently arrested him earlier today. Leon said Milius and his wife want me to defend him, and Leon made it pretty clear that *he* wants me to defend him. Leon said it doesn't make sense that Milius would kill a girl that was making him a fortune, and he says Milius is insisting he's innocent. Leon told them the fee would be a million up front plus expenses, and they apparently were okay with that figure. They want an answer within forty-eight hours." I looked at Caroline. "What do you think? Do I call Leon back and tell him no, or should we consider it? It's a lot of money."

"How long will it take? A year?" she asked.

"Depends on which judge we draw and what his or her docket is like. It also depends on Milius. I can move for a speedy trial if that's what he wants, but you know how it is. Most defendants want it to drag on as long as possible, hoping a key witness will die or evidence will get lost. It could take longer than a year."

"How much time will you have to actually spend in Nashville?"

"I don't know, babe. Leon says Milius has a private jet, and I can negotiate being home as much as possible. Charlie and Jack are both living there, so I can hire Charlie—if she's willing—and let her handle a lot of the pre-trial work. I can hire other lawyers from Nashville if I need to. If it winds up going to trial, which it probably will since he's paying out so much money, then I'll have to spend some time down there. But at this point, I don't have any way of knowing how long the trial will take because I don't know anything about the case."

"What if Caroline gets sick?"

The question came from my sister, Sarah, a raven-haired, strong-jawed woman a year older than me who was sitting near Caroline on the couch. She was the only adult in the room who was completely sober because she'd had so many problems with drug and alcohol abuse in the past that she didn't allow herself to drink. She didn't mind, however, that the rest of us imbibed occasionally.

"She's already sick," I said. "And that's why we're talking about it. If it wasn't for the cancer, I don't think there would be much question as to whether I'd take a case like this."

"What if she gets worse?" Sarah said.

I shrugged my shoulders and looked at Caroline.

"I hate to put this on you, but it's your call," I said. "If you don't want me to go, I won't, and I won't regret it in the least. If you want me to do it, I'll do it."

"That isn't fair, Dad," my daughter, Lilly, who was a twenty-four-year old clone of Caroline with the exception that her eyes were blue, said with a slight slur. Lilly was the pacifist in the family. She avoided confrontation like she avoided communicable diseases, so I was surprised when she spoke up, but like the rest of us, she'd been drinking.

"Why is it not fair?" I said. "She's the one who has cancer. If she doesn't want me to take the case, all she has to do is say so. I'm willing to abide by whatever decision she makes."

"Just tell them thanks but no thanks," Lilly said. "If the circumstances were different, if Mom wasn't sick, then we could have a discussion about whether you being away for what could be an extended period of time would be a good idea. But she *is* sick, and I think it's selfish and egotistical of you to even consider it."

I felt my jaw drop involuntarily and took a sip of wine.

"Wow," I said. "Selfish and egotistical? Because I have the audacity to consider earning a million-dollar fee that will go a long, long way toward providing for my family for many years to come? That's a bit harsh, don't you think?"

"You don't have to 'provide for your family' anymore," Lilly said, using her fingers to place quotation marks around the phrase. "Randy and I are fine. I have a good job, and he's in medical school. Jack is about to graduate from law school. All you have to worry about is you and Mom. You guys have money, don't you? Do you really need a million dollars?"

"Did you hear what you just said? Are you listening to yourself? Who the hell doesn't need a million dollars?"

Caroline stood and raised a hand.

"Stop," she said. "I won't have raised voices in the house on Christmas Eve." She looked around the room at each of us with tears welling in her eyes. "I love all of you so much, and I regret that we have to go through this...this *experience* with cancer. Lilly, I appreciate what you said, and I understand how you feel. And you're right. Your father doesn't need to provide for you and Jack anymore. You've both done a wonderful job of being able to take care of yourselves. But you also know how your father is. I don't think him taking a case like this has anything at all to do with money. From what he said a few minutes ago, he smells injustice, and when he smells injustice, he wants to do something about it. It's an important part of who he is, what he's become. It's what he does, and I admire him for it. And as far as me getting sicker, getting worse, even dying, well, I just can't accept that we have to live our lives or make our choices based on such a huge uncertainty.

"I realize I might not be here next Christmas, and I know all of you think about it. It's there, always, in the back of our minds. But you know what? I might be here ten Christmases from now. I read all the time about women with metastatic breast cancer who are still alive after ten, fifteen years. The treatments are better than they used to be, and I'm young and strong and, for the most part, healthy. So I say we take the cancer considera-tion completely out of the picture and make a decision based on what we think is best for everyone in this room.

"Jack, I'm sure your dad will involve you in the case as much as he can since you're in Nashville, and the expe-rience you'll gain in a high-profile murder case will be extremely valuable to you. Charlie, he's already said he'd like to hire you, which I assume will mean you'll earn a fairly significant fee for yourself and gain some useful experience. Lilly, you and Randy and Sarah and the kids can keep me company when Joe is away. It'll give us an excuse to get together more often. And say what you will about money, a million dollars isn't an amount you can simply ignore. It could eventually benefit Grace or Joey or any children Jack might have. Your dad and I have been on both sides of the poverty line during our marriage. Back when he was in law school, we had two children and were living off the measly salary I was making at a dance school in Knoxville. We got through it, but I have to tell you that given the choice between wealth and poverty, I choose wealth."

She paused for a few seconds and shook her head. "I don't think I've ever said that many words at one time in my entire life." She looked at me, smiled, and nodded her head several times.

"What?" I said.

"Go to Nashville," she said. "Do what you do. Go be a hero."

CHAPTER 5

As the jet descended from an overcast sky toward the private airstrip, I looked out the window into a soupy fog. Paul Milius owned a fifteen-hundred-acre estate called "Xanadu" outside Franklin, about thirty miles south of Nashville. I didn't know it when I first flew over it that day, but the estate included a couple small lakes, surrounded by rolling pastures fenced with white rails and populated by more than fifty quarter horses. There were also patches of woods; several creeks and ponds; an airstrip; a massive, thirty-room, twenty-thousand-square-foot home that looked like a palace; a five-thousand-square-foot guest house that would be my home when I was in Nashville; two tennis courts; a golf driving range; an indoor-outdoor swimming pool; an airplane hangar; and a garage that contained fifteen vintage and antique automobiles, collectively worth around $2 million.

Milius's wife, the country music icon Lana Raines, had dispatched their luxurious Gulfstream 550 jet to pick me up at the Tri-Cities airport, five miles from my home, at eight in the morning. I was the only passenger, but a pretty, sassy, young brunette named Becky acted as flight attendant and offered to attend to my every need. She seemed genuinely disappointed when I had no needs. The flight had taken about forty-five minutes, so taking into account the loss of an hour because we'd crossed into the Central Standard Time zone, I was arriving in Nashville fifteen minutes earlier than I'd left the Tri-Cities.

As soon as the jet rolled to a stop on the runway, Becky ushered me out the door, and a uniformed chauffeur who introduced himself as David held open the rear, passenger-side door of a navy-blue Mercedes S63 AMG sedan. The car drove down the runway and eventually wound up at the front door of the mansion. I climbed out of the car without waiting for the chauffeur to open the door for me and walked up to the house. The door opened before I could knock or ring a bell.

"Mr. Dillard? Welcome."

The shapely young woman who spoke to me was wearing a pair of what looked to be very expensive blue jeans (although I'm not particularly knowledgeable about such things), a white blouse that appeared to be made of silk, a bright, multi-colored scarf of the same material that hung loosely around her neck, and black shoes with spiked heels. Her hair was thick and shiny and black and wavy and tumbled down her shoulders like a waterfall. Her face was attractive—not beautiful, not striking in any particular way—but easy to look at. Her skin was tanned and smooth and had a sheen to it, as though it had been moisturized recently.

"Follow me, please," she said without introducing herself, and she turned and started walking through the most spectacular home I had ever set foot in. Everything seemed to glisten: chandeliers, shiny granite floors, elegant wood moldings, vaulted ceilings, expensive paintings and tapestries. As I looked around the place, it put me in mind of how a Roman emperor or a Colombian drug lord might live, and I wondered whether the kitchen and bathroom faucets and fixtures might be plated in twenty-four-carat gold. But there was something else that struck me about the place. It was so opulent, so gaudy, that it didn't seem real, and it certainly didn't seem like a home. There was nothing cozy or comfortable about it. It was cold.

"That's a beautiful scarf," I said as we continued past magnificence on all sides. "Is it silk?"

"Yes," she said. "It was a gift from Lana."

"I didn't catch your name," I said.

She glanced back over her shoulder and said, "I'm Lisa. Lisa Trent. I'm Lana's personal assistant. Are you going to get Mr. Milius out of jail today?"

"I'll try," I said. "Depends on the judge."

"I've heard you're very good at what you do."

"Really? Who's talking about me?"

"Lana, mostly. She says she knows one of your best friends, and he's told her about all the exciting things you've done. You've lived quite an interesting life, haven't you?"

"I don't know about that. Seems like it's been pretty simple to me. How long have you known Mrs. Milius?"

"Not long, actually. I've only been working here for about a month."

"Where are you from, Lisa?"

"I grew up in a little place called Dayton, Tennessee."

"Dayton? Down around Chattanooga, the place where they held the Scopes trial?"

"That's it, the monkey trial."

"Which side do you come down on? Creation or evolution?"

"Oh, I'm a creationist through and through. What about you?"

"I'd have to say I'm a mixture. All this was created somehow and evolved into what it is now. It's still evolving."

"Into what?"

"Beg your pardon?"

"What's it evolving into, Mr. Dillard? Where do you think it ends?"

"I have absolutely no idea. I just hope it doesn't blow up any time soon."

We rounded a corner and entered a huge, opulent sunroom/atrium decorated with palm trees, ferns, and dozens of species of tropical plants. Sitting at a white wicker table about fifteen feet from the entrance was a woman dressed in a kimono, red silk covered with pink blossoms. She was lifting a dainty, white porcelain cup to her lips as we approached, and she looked me up and down intently, the same way a man sizing me up before a fistfight might look at me. Her face was just a touch fuller than I remembered during her heyday, but Lana Raines-Milius was as striking as ever. Her red hair glowed like fire, her cobalt-blue eyes were intense, her lips were sensual, and her skin was smooth and creamy white. Everything about the woman suggested sexual allure. I knew from doing some research that she was thirty-three years old, had sold sixty million records by the time she was twenty-five, and had famously quit the industry at the ripe old age of twenty-seven. I walked up to the table and reached out my hand. She remained seated and continued to eye me.

"Leon didn't tell me you were tall, dark, and handsome," she said in a smooth, southern lilt as she took my hand and squeezed.

"He probably hasn't noticed. It's nice to meet you, Mrs. Milius."

"Call me Lana, please," she said. "You've lightened my bank account by a million dollars. It's the least you can do."

"Fine then. It's nice to meet you, Lana."

"Your eyes are beautiful," she said. "They're the same color blue as mine."

"You're very kind."

"I trust your flight was satisfactory."

"It was. Thank you for sending the plane."

"What can I offer you? Have you had breakfast?"

"I have, thank you."

"Tea then? Coffee? Juice?"

"Coffee, please. Black."

"Lisa, would you tell Michael to bring Mr. Dillard a cup of black coffee, please? And tell him I'd like some fresh tea. I'll catch up with you a little later."

Lisa excused herself and left the room through the same door we'd come in.

I watched her go and said, "Nice girl. Pretty, too."

"Everybody's pretty in Nashville," Lana said. "Fans won't pay millions to watch ugly people perform. It's the same in Hollywood and New York, London, Calcutta, doesn't matter. It's show business, it's glamorous, it's fairyland. Nothing is real, and nothing is ugly with the exception of the truth."

"So it's strictly about appearances?" I said. "I thought success in Nashville was supposed to be about the quality of the music."

"Lots of people can make good music," she said. "Lots of people can sing. Tens of thousands of them. Only the pretty ones get paid, though. If someone pays eighty dollars for a concert ticket and they come to watch and live through the performer vicariously, they don't want to be ugly. They want to be beautiful for a few hours. If they wanted to be ugly, they'd just go in the bathroom and watch themselves in the mirror."

I thought about the country performers I'd listened to and watched on television, especially over the past few years, and all I could do was nod. All the most popular country singers were beautiful, even the women.

"So that's all it takes?" I asked. "Beauty and a little talent?"

"A healthy dose of drive and a treacherous heart are distinct advantages, but even with beauty, talent, drive, and treachery, making it big is still a lottery. Luck is the most important part of the process."

A short, chubby, balding black man appeared just then, wearing a white coat and shirt and black pants. His hair was receding and starting to gray, and his cheeks were full and round. He walked slowly and carried a rectangular tray at waist level.

"My goodness, Michael," Lana said. "Could you move any slower? The man asked for coffee. Where have you been? Did you have to pick and grind the beans?"

"Had to grow 'em first, Mizz Lana. Got 'em here as quick as I could. So whacha need now, missy? Wants me ta sing fo' da gentleman? Wants me ta dance? Wants me ta *smile* at him?"

For a second, I thought I'd been transported in time to Tara, or maybe to the set of a bad Al Jolson vaudeville act.

"Stop it," Lana said. "Mr. Dillard, meet Michael Pillston, our chef. He's a well-educated and articulate man, but he's angry because his assistant—a woman *he* hired, mind you—has called in sick today, and he is forced into the lowly position of having to serve us. Poor baby. Michael, this is Joe Dillard. We've hired him to represent Paul."

"I know," the chef said in a deep bass. He turned to me, bowed slightly, and gave me a cross between a smile and a smirk. "Welcome to Xanadu, Mr. Dillard. I hope it isn't your downfall." And with that, he turned sharply on his heel like a solider and marched out of the room. The slow gait was gone.

I'd been away from home for just over an hour, and already I'd ridden on a private jet and met Paul Milius's pilot, copilot and a stewardess named Becky. I'd landed in a paradise called "Xanadu" and met a chauffeur who introduced himself as David, a country star named Lana Raines-Milius, her personal assistant, Lisa, and a grumpy chef named Michael.

"Wow," I said, picking up my coffee and looking at Lana. "This place is really...interesting."

"Oh, honey," she said as her lips curled into a mischievous smile. "You ain't seen nothing yet."

CHAPTER 6

Paul Milius wasn't nearly as pretty as his wife, although his physical appearance had undergone some fairly significant changes in recent years based on older photos I'd seen of him on the Internet. His nose was smaller and straighter than it had been in early photos, and his hairline had moved forward and smoothed out. His teeth, of course, were perfect. He had the face of a man with loads of money and vanity to match.

Milius was a large, somewhat lumbering man with mid-length, curly black hair, dark eyes, and a broad face. I met him in the visiting room at the Metro-Davidson Correctional Center in Nashville, about ninety minutes after I got off the plane in Franklin, and the first thing I did was look at his hands. I couldn't help it. Could he have strangled a young woman with them? They were formidable. The answer was yes.

The look on Milius's face was a mixture of desperation, confusion, and fear, similar, I suppose, to an animal caught in a trap. The problem Milius faced was that he couldn't get out of the trap even if he gnawed off an arm or a leg. We went through the formalities of introduction and a bit of small talk before I said, "Your wife paid me, Mr. Milius, but I need to be certain that you're comfortable with me representing you before I appear in court with you."

"I'm comfortable with it," he said.

"Do you know anything at all about me?"

"I know a lot about you, Mr. Dillard. My wife is thorough, sometimes to the point of obsession. I know how old you are, how many kids you have, and where you went to high school, undergrad, and law school. I know how many cases you've tried and your record in court. I know you've been a defense lawyer, a prosecutor, and now you're a defense lawyer again. I know you're a decorated Army veteran, and I know you were a Ranger. I know your parents are dead and your wife is ill, and I'm extremely sorry about that. You have two grown children and one grandchild. Your house and land are paid for, you're not in debt, and you don't gamble, don't do drugs, don't drink much, and don't smoke. You pay your taxes on time. I also know you most likely killed several men who tried to assassinate you and your family a couple years ago at your home, and you were probably at least indirectly responsible for the disappearance of a man named John Lipscomb, whom I was acquainted with, by the way, and despised. You aren't afraid to stand up to authority, you aren't afraid to bend rules when you think they need to be bent, and you aren't afraid of cops or big cases, although I believe this is probably by far the biggest case you've ever taken on. As far as I'm concerned, you seem to be just what I need."

I could have done without the references to John Lipscomb and the Colombian *sicarios* Leon Bates and I had killed, but since it was all true, there wasn't much I could say.

"Your turn," Milius said. "Tell me what you know about me."

"I made some inquiries," I said. I suppose I could have reached into my briefcase and pulled out a file, but since he'd rattled off all the information about me without looking at anything, I decided to show off and do the same.

"Forty-four years old, married to Lana Raines-Milius for fifteen years, no children. Son of Eugene and Daphne Milius. Born in Queens, New York, moved to Nashville when you were sixteen. Only child. Your father, who was a pharmaceutical rep, died of a stroke when you were eighteen. Your mother is still alive, a retired chemistry professor, and lives near you outside Franklin. You graduated high school with honors and then graduated from Belmont College in three years. Majored in business management. Went to work immediately for Steelhead Records in the promotions department. Worked for four other record companies before you decided to start your own label when you were twenty-seven years old. Gathered a small group of investors, incorporated offshore, and went to it. You've done well and are responsible for 'democratizing'—a phrase you introduced to the world—the country music industry through the use of social media. Estimated personal net worth is $450 million and growing. Reputation as a tough negotiator but no serious accusations of dishonesty. Borderline diabetic, never been arrested."

"Until now," he said with a sigh. "This is absolutely unbelievable. I don't know how anyone could think I killed Kasey. I loved her like a daughter."

"We don't need to get into any specifics right now," I said. "Too many eyes and ears in these visiting booths. I'll try to get the judge to set a bond when we go to court in a couple hours. If he does, we'll talk somewhere more private. In the meantime, the judge will ask you at the arraignment whether you understand what you're charged with. Do you?"

"They charged me with murder, didn't they?"

"Second-degree. Second-degree murder is pretty simple. It's defined by the statute as a knowing killing of another."

"Ridiculous. I didn't kill her. The district attorney is a friend of mine, for God's sake."

I held up my hand to silence him. "Not now," I said. "I need to tell you that second-degree murder is a Class A felony in Tennessee. It carries a minimum of fifteen years and a maximum of sixty years. Since you've never been arrested, you'll probably qualify as what's known as a mitigated offender. That means the minimum sentence for you would be thirteen and a half years, and the maximum would be twenty-five years. If you plead and take the minimum, you'd be eligible for release on parole after serving a little less than three years. I'm not saying the parole board would release you the first time you came up—they most likely wouldn't release you until you've served at least ten years—but it's possible. Do you understand?"

"You're saying I could plead guilty to murder and serve less than three years? Is that what I'm hearing?"

It's funny how people hear what they want to hear sometimes. I'd just told him he'd most likely serve ten years and he'd heard three.

"I'm saying it's possible, not probable. Depends on the prosecutor and the judge and whether you even want to consider a plea. Since your wife paid me so much money, I'm operating under the assumption that we'll be going to trial. Besides, if the prosecutor wants to stick it to you and the judge is on his side, you could plead guilty and draw a twenty-five-year sentence."

"You're making me dizzy," he said.

"Sorry. It's a little complicated, but you'll figure it out eventually. For now, when the judge asks you if you understand the charge against you, just say yes. We'll plead not guilty, and I'll ask for bond. I'm assuming you can handle a significant bond? Say a million dollars?"

Milius nodded.

"Do you have a passport?"

"Yes."

"You'll have to surrender it. What about a trial date? Do you want to be tried as quickly as possible, or do you want to drag it out as long as we can?"

"I want this behind me as soon as possible."

"Good. I'll see you in court. And remember this very, very clearly, Mr. Milius. You don't have any friends at this jail. If anyone wants to talk to you about your case, they're either trying to set you up to extort you, or they'll make a deal with the prosecution and testify against you. So keep your mouth shut."

CHAPTER 7

Based on my experience with high-profile cases, I knew Paul Milius's arraignment would most likely be a circus, but I was unprepared for the scope of the idiocy on display outside and inside the criminal court building in downtown Nashville. David, Paul Milius's driver, had driven me to the jail and was now driving me to the courthouse for the arraignment. I had refused to ride in the backseat and was sitting next to him in the front.

"There's something I need to tell you," David said.

"Yeah? What's that?"

"It's about Mr. Milius. The police have already talked to me, and I had to tell them the truth."

"Okay. Let's hear it."

"That night, the night this happened, was the same night as the Country Music Television Artists of the Year show at the City Center. I drove Mr. Milius to the show, and then I drove him to the after-party at a restaurant downtown. He came out of the restaurant around two in the morning and asked me to drive him to the Plaza Hotel, which is where they found Kasey Cartwright's body the next morning. I dropped him off in front of the hotel, and he told me to go on home, that he'd see me the next morning."

"And?"

"That's it. I dropped him off and went home. The next morning, he walked out the back door at six-thirty sharp, just like he does every Monday through Saturday. I took him to the office. The night before wasn't even mentioned. I just thought you should know. It might be a problem."

"Thanks," I said.

I let out a soft whistle as we approached the six-story A.A. Birch Building on Second Avenue near the Cumberland River. There were news vans and trucks everywhere. We turned onto James Robertson Parkway, and David pulled over in front of the huge courthouse.

"You probably should ask somebody about a back way or a side way out when you're finished," he said. "You have my cell number. Just call and I'll pick you up."

I got out of the Mercedes and followed the crowd into the building, glad to be anonymous, at least for a little while longer. I went through security and made my way up to the sixth floor to Courtroom 6B. When I opened the door, I saw the room was packed with reporters and cameras. Court wasn't due to start for another twenty minutes, and there were no lawyers standing or sitting beyond the bar, so I closed the door and walked to the other end of the hall. I leaned against the wall and watched from a distance for the next fifteen minutes while people went in and out of the courtroom door and milled around in the hallway. Five minutes before Paul Milius's arraignment was scheduled to begin, I walked into the courtroom and strode straight to the front. A lanky, early-forties man in a dark suit and a young woman were sitting at the table to my right, near the jury box. I set my briefcase down on the table to my left and listened to the raised whispers and low murmurs behind me.

"That's him. That's Dillard. I heard Milius hired Joe Dillard, didn't believe it. No, no, he's from northeast of Knoxville. The mountains, yeah, Johnson City, Bristol, Kingsport, Jonesborough, all those little towns. Used to be a prosecutor. Yeah, a real brawler from what they say. Quite a reputation."

I felt someone looming to my right and turned.

"Pennington Frye," the man said, holding out his hand, which I took. He was the same man who had been sitting at the prosecutor's table a moment before. He looked like images I'd seen of Ichabod Crane, all lanky and gangly with a sharp widow's peak.

"Joe Dillard."

"Would you describe yourself as famous or infamous?"

"I'd describe myself as a lawyer doing a job. Would you describe yourself as Ronnie Johnson's top gun?" Ronnie Johnson was the district attorney general of Davidson County, which comprised the Twentieth Judicial District in Tennessee. I'd never met Johnson or Frye, although I'd heard Johnson speak at a district attorney general's convention back when I was the DA of the First Judicial District and had been impressed.

"You might say that," Frye said. "I handle the violent felonies and the high-profile cases."

"You must be a pretty good trial lawyer then."

"I like to think so."

"How's the judge?"

"Judge Graves? I suppose he's fine. I haven't heard anything to the contrary."

"I mean how is it working with him? I assume you've tried cases in front of him."

"He's an arrogant, pompous tyrant. Aren't they all?"

I smiled and nodded. No matter how things went from there, at least Frye and I shared a low opinion of judges. I looked over at the table to my right. The young woman sitting there was scowling at me.

"Who's your friend?" I said to Frye.

"Dee Dee Black. Victim-witness coordinator. She doesn't like defense lawyers."

"It's a big club."

Just then a door opened to the right of the judge's bench, and a uniformed bailiff called court to order. Judge Ian Graves, mid-fifties and looking squat and Irish and irritable, walked in, black robe flowing.

"*State versus Paul Milius*, case number three-seven-six-five-five-four for arraignment," the judge said. "The State of Tennessee is represented by Mister Pennington Frye, and the defendant is represented by…who?"

"Joe Dillard, Judge," I said. "I'm from Washington County, usually practice in the First Judicial District."

"Ah, then you knew my friend Len Green," he said. Judge Leonard Green had been perhaps the most perfect example of a son of a bitch I'd ever known before he was murdered several years back.

"I did. I tried many cases in front of him."

"He was a good man," Judge Graves said. "I miss him."

"You're the only person on the planet who misses him," I wanted to say. Instead, I said, "Yes, sir."

"Bring in the defendant," the judge said, and less than ten seconds later Paul Milius, handcuffed, waist-chained, shackled, wearing striped coveralls and flanked by two sheriff's deputies, walked in.

"Excuse me, Judge," I said, "but isn't this overkill? Shackles and a waist chain? Do you typically allow defendants to be treated this way in your courtroom?"

Graves glared at me over his reading glasses.

"Defendants accused of murdering children get special treatment," he said.

"So the presumption of innocence is just…what? A meaningless phrase? This is a prominent businessman in the community—the nation, for that matter. He's a philanthropist who has donated millions to charities. He's never been arrested, never even had a traffic ticket from what I've been able to gather. And as far as I know, he hasn't yet been convicted in this case."

"Security at the courthouse is handled by the Davidson County Sheriff's Department, Mr. Dillard," the judge said as Milius stepped up beside me at the defense table. "I don't interfere with how he conducts his business, and he doesn't interfere with how I conduct mine. If you don't like it, take it up with Sheriff Hightower. And I'd advise you to watch your tone when you're addressing this court."

My "tone" in addressing the court, in fact my entire little speech, was designed with a purpose in mind: to let the court know that I wasn't a pushover, wasn't a brown-noser, and would vigorously and zealously represent Paul Milius. There is a fine line between zealous representation and obnoxious representation, however, and lawyers who don't recognize the line and who cross it are, for the most part, ineffective. But I've always felt it important to establish my identity early on in a case, whether it be in front of a judge or an opposing lawyer or a witness or a jury, and I've always felt my identity needed to be one of strength and competence, even if I was scared out of my wits and completely unsure of what I was doing.

"I meant no disrespect to the court," I said, at least somewhat sincerely.

Judge Graves looked at his clerk and said, "Pass me the file, please." He opened it, took out a copy of the indictment, and handed it to a bailiff, who walked it over to me. "Mr. Milius," the judge said, "you've been indicted by the Davidson County grand jury on one count of second-degree murder. Have you had a chance to speak with Mr. Dillard prior to this hearing?"

"Yes," Milius said.

"Did Mr. Dillard explain the charge to you?"

"Yes."

"Do you understand the charge against you?"

"I do."

"How does your client plead, Mr. Dillard?"

"Not guilty."

"Do you wish to have the indictment read into the record?"

"We waive the formal reading."

"I suppose you want to talk about bail," the judge said.

"We ask for half a million, and we can post cash," I said. "Mr. Milius has lived and worked in this area for most of his life and has strong ties here. His wife and mother are here. His business is headquartered here. Up until this charge, he had an impeccable reputation, and, as I said earlier, he has absolutely no criminal record. I haven't seen all the state's evidence, but I understand the case is largely circumstantial. I could bring any number of witnesses to court, including state legislators, to testify as to his character and reputation. Mr. Milius is willing to surrender his passport and will not leave the area until the case is resolved."

"Mr. Frye?" the judge said.

"The state asks that he remain in custody," Frye said. "Mr. Milius is a wealthy man, which means he's a flight risk. He's facing a long sentence after he's convicted of this heinous murder of an innocent, young girl, and we believe he's likely to flee."

"Bail is set in the amount of $1 million, cash," Judge Graves said. "I want him to surrender his passport. What about a trial date? Mr. Dillard?"

"As quickly as possible, Judge. I'd like it on the record that we're asserting our right to a speedy trial."

"So noted."

Graves turned and huddled with his clerk for a couple minutes and then turned back to us.

"April twenty-fifth," he said. "Which means you better get your experts lined up in a hurry and get all your information exchanged without having to come in here and argue in front of me. Any objections from anyone?"

The question was met with silence.

"Good. So unless something comes up in the meantime, I'll see you folks in just short of four months, and we'll have ourselves a trial. I'm sure it'll be loads of fun."

I stood along with everyone else while the judge strutted out of the room. The deputies led Milius out. He would be taken back to the jail and released in a few hours, after his bond was posted and the paperwork completed. When the door closed behind Milius, I turned to look at the pack of jackals that called themselves reporters, and then turned to Pennington Frye.

"Is there a way out of here without having to deal with the press?" I asked.

He looked at the crowded courtroom and then back at me.

"Sure," he said. "Follow me."

PART II

CHAPTER 8

Charlie Story, a beautiful young lady whose hair was the same color as my wife's, sat looking across her desk at me. My son, Jack, dark-haired like me but brown-eyed like his mom, was in a chair to my left. We were in Charlie's office, a nice little renovated house off Edgehill Avenue in Nashville not far from the Vanderbilt campus. They had driven down from our home near Johnson City early that morning while I was flying down, talking to Lana and Paul, and going to the arraignment. As Caroline had suggested early on, I had hired Charlie to help me with the defense of Paul Milius, and I'd given her a retainer of $50,000. She was to bill against the retainer at $200 an hour, a relatively low rate for lawyers but one that was fair since she was somewhat new to the game. I'd paid for her attention for two hundred and fifty hours, which bought me a lot of legwork and a lot of research. After that, if I needed more, I'd have to refill the tank.

Jack was still in law school, but he was about to begin his last semester and was cruising. I'd offered him fifty dollars an hour to do investigative work, paralegal work, and whatever else we needed. He seemed satisfied with both the money and the opportunity to get into something real.

"It's an uphill battle, but I've seen worse," I said. "I talked to Pennington Frye—he's the assistant district attorney who's handling the case—and he said they have a small piece of skin that was lifted from between the victim's teeth. The DNA test says the skin belonged to Paul before he apparently smacked her in the mouth and left it there. They can put him at her hotel near the time she was murdered through his driver, and I wouldn't be surprised if they have video of Paul coming and going through the lobby. They must have more, too. I've seen prosecutors indict on nearly nothing, but this is a high-profile case. They won't want to be embarrassed."

"What does Milius have to say about the skin?" Jack asked.

"I haven't gotten into it very deeply with him," I said. "I want to talk to him when his wife isn't around and I'm not worried about someone eavesdropping on the conversation. I'm not sure how many people he has working at the house, but it seems to be quite a few. I'll talk to him later, but I want you to take a run at him first, Charlie."

"Me? Why me?"

"He apparently likes younger women. Smile at him and be nice, but ask him some tough questions."

Charlie smiled and said, "Love to."

I was happy for Charlie. She'd been through a terribly difficult time a year earlier after she found a fortune in gold in a cave on a piece of land that a neighbor had willed to her. She later learned that the gold had originally belonged to a gangster from Philadelphia back in the thirties, and eventually both her father and uncle were killed by the gangster's son. She'd finally had the cave's entrance blown up to seal the gold in and had moved away. She'd traveled around for a while before settling in Nashville, mostly, I think, because of her feelings for Jack. She was renting a little farmhouse outside Mt. Pleasant, had enough land to keep her horse and her uncle's dog, and was building her own law practice. All those things made her tough and resilient in my eyes, and I admired people who were tough and resilient.

"I'll set it up," I said. "It'd probably be best if you talk to him here. He'll want you to come to him, but I'd rather you do it on your own turf."

"Anything besides the skin between the teeth?" she asked.

"Talk to him about his wife, how well they get along. Ask about problems in the marriage, things like that. It appears that he spent the night, or part of the night, in a hotel room with the victim, who was an eighteen-year-old girl. He didn't get there until two in the morning, so I seriously doubt that his wife knew where he was. Even if she did know, I doubt she approved, so get what you can out of him about that. Talk to him about the girl. See what his reactions are, whether you feel like he was in love, in lust, or whether their relationship was primarily about business. Remember that if he had anything to do with her death, about 90 percent of what he tells you will be a lie."

"I'm getting better at it," she said.

"At what?"

"Listening to lies. And recognizing them when I hear them. It seems to me that being good at this profession is all about learning to deal with liars."

"Don't get too confident about thinking you can recognize them," I said. "I've been doing this for almost three decades, and it's still hit or miss for me."

"What about me?" Jack said. "What can I do?"

"You can start with the music business. Find people in the profession that she was close to, people associated with her record label—producers, musicians, singers, anybody and everybody. Try to get a handle on what went on at that CMT show, whether anybody saw or heard anything unusual. You both need to understand that we're behind the cops. We have to catch up, and hopefully, we can find a way to get a step or two ahead of them eventually. They have more resources than we do, but once they make an arrest, they tend to move on to other cases until it's time for the trial. We have some time. We just have to work hard. We also have to start thinking about the SODDI defense."

"SODDI defense?" Charlie said, raising her eyebrows.

"Some Other Dude Done It," Jack said with a smile. "I heard it plenty of times when I was younger."

"If our client didn't do it, we need to be able to give the jury some viable alternatives," I said. "It's similar to conducting our own police investigation. The main difference is that we exclude our client at the beginning and don't even consider that he might be guilty."

"But what do you think, Dad?" Jack said. "Do you think he killed her?"

"He says he didn't. There is evidence that suggests otherwise, although not an overwhelming amount at this point. At this stage in the game, I've been paid $1 million to believe my client, so that's what I choose to do."

"And if at some point you change your mind?"

"I'm not giving them a refund, so I guess I swallow it and do the job."

"And while Charlie is talking to Milius and I'm running around Nashville, what are you going to be doing?"

"The first thing I'm going to do is take Lana Milius to dinner and try to find out where she stands on all of this," I said. "I talked to her briefly before the arraignment, but I want to pin her down on some things. Then I'm going to get some sleep, get up tomorrow, and spend as much time as I can talking to the household staff. Like I said, I'm not sure how many there are, but I want to talk to every one of them. I got the sense that some of them are very deeply involved in the Miliuses' lives. As soon as I'm finished, I'm going to get back on that fancy private plane and go home and find out everything I can about Kasey Cartwright."

"How long are you going to stay? A week?"

"Nah, I'll be out of here in two days. One if possible."

"Why?" Jack said. "I mean, why so soon?"

"Because I already miss your mother."

CHAPTER 9

Not a word was being said, but the air seemed to be alive, buzzing with tension as Lana Milius prepared for the evening out she was scheduled to have with Joe Dillard. Paul had just arrived at Xanadu after having been released from jail. He walked through the bedroom toward his bathroom while Lana sat at a vanity mirror applying moisturizer to her face.

"So how was jail, honey?" Lana said in her most sarcastic tone. "Did you meet any singers? Any potential money-makers?"

"Shut your hole, Lana. I don't feel like listening to you right now."

"Speaking of holes, how is yours? Did any of those big, mean boys explore you? Did they stretch it?"

"I'm serious, Lana. Shut it or I'm gonna rip your head off."

"Then you'll be facing two murder charges."

Paul walked into his bathroom and semi-closed the door behind him. Lana, seeing it was still open, raised her voice.

"You lied to me again, Paulie," she called. "You didn't tell me you went to her room that night. You also failed to mention that you slapped her across the face."

Paul appeared in the doorway, a towel draped over his shoulder and a toothbrush hanging from his mouth.

"I went to her room to apologize for the things *you* said to her at the party," he said.

"I don't need you making apologies for me. And besides, what I said to her wasn't all that bad."

"You called her a chubby, no-talent wannabe who looked like a bloodhound and sang like one, too. You sang it to the tune of 'Happy Birthday.'"

"I thought that was kind of cute. It was mild, too."

"She was a beautiful girl, Lana, and she made—"

"You had insurance on her, didn't you?"

"What? How could you say a thing like that?"

"Well, you did, didn't you?"

"Of course."

"How much?"

"I'm not having this conversation with you."

Lana got up from the stool where she was sitting and walked toward him.

"Yes you are, Paul. You're having this conversation. You killed her. Now how much was she worth?"

"I killed her? I can't believe this. You really think I killed Kasey."

"You *did* kill her. You killed her the minute you started following her around like a heartsick teenager. And if you hadn't gotten yourself tossed out of the room, you'd probably have been lying up there dead, too."

"What do you mean by that?" Paul said as he took another step toward his wife. "What exactly are you saying?"

"I'm saying if you'd been there you might have been killed, too. I'm saying you're probably lucky to be alive."

"No, no. You said I killed her the minute I started following her around like a heartsick puppy. What is that supposed to mean? Did you have something to do with this, Lana?"

Lana folded her arms and stared at him. "What did she say to you that made you slap her, sweetheart? Did she make fun of the size of your wee-wee? Did she use Zeus's name in vain? Did she insult your Greekness?"

Paul placed a thick finger on Lana's nose and pushed.

"If I find out you had Kasey killed, I'll bury you," he said.

"Why don't you just kill me now?" Lana said. "It would be such fun. You'd have to figure out what to do with my body and then hide everything from the police. I know...you could take me out by the stables and bury me in that soft ground."

Paul removed his finger from her nose, straightened up, and turned his back on her.

"It'd be the right place for you," he said. "Buried out there among the other black widows and the horse manure." The door slammed with a bang.

"Black widows," Lana said quietly as she turned back to her dressing table. "Perfect."

CHAPTER 10

A few hours after I left Charlie and Jack and after I'd called Caroline and talked to her for a little while, I found myself in a limousine owned by Paul and Lana. Lana had her own driver, a silver-haired man she introduced as Bennett. Bennett the driver picked me up at the guesthouse at 8:00 p.m. sharp, pulled around to the back of the big house, and Lana climbed into the seat next to me.

She looked damned-near stunning, and I immediately felt underdressed, although I have to admit I wasn't all that concerned about it. She was a star, after all, and I was, as Leon Bates had put it, a ham-and-egger. She was wearing a waist-length black coat that was puffy at the shoulders and probably cost twice what most people make in a week. I didn't know anything about fashion or labels and never will, but Lana's clothes, her makeup, her earrings, her necklace, her handbag, her shoes, her watch, all of it screamed one word: *expensive*. Her skirt was thigh-length and revealed long, slim, shapely legs beneath sheer, dark hose. The front of her coat was as low cut as the cream-colored V-necked top beneath the coat. I had to force myself not to look at the spot where the V-neck naturally led the eye. Her skin was shimmering, and she smelled like a field of wildflowers after a summer rain.

"Good evening, Lana," I said after she'd settled in and Bennett the driver had closed the door behind her.

"Good evening, Mr. Dillard," she said.

"Call me Joe," I said. "I lightened your bank account by $1 million. It's the least you can do."

She smiled and nodded. "Good evening, Joe."

"I'm a happily married man, Lana, and I don't mean this any other way than honestly. I was just thinking that you look damned-near stunning, but I'm going to have to remove the 'damned-near' from the description. You look stunning."

"Why, thank you, Mr. Dill—Joe. A woman never grows tired of hearing things like that, especially when the compliment is, as you say, an honest one."

Bennett was pulling away from the house, and I looked around at the grounds. It was dark, but the place was still lit up for the holidays and glowed like a city skyline.

"This is beautiful," I said. "Do you ever find yourself taking it for granted?"

"What an unusual question," Lana said. "Why would you ask?"

"I don't know," I said. "I didn't mean any offense. It's just that since my wife got sick, and especially since her cancer metastasized last year, I try to remind myself on a regular basis not to take things that are good or beautiful for granted. Doesn't matter whether it's someone I love or a red rose petal or a clear night when the sky is full of stars or a beautiful display of Christmas lights like this one. I try to take more deep breaths, to go slower, to not worry and fret about so many things."

"So your wife's illness has turned you into a philosopher?"

"I'm no philosopher, Lana, believe me. I just think maybe it's made me more introspective." I suddenly felt embarrassed and said, "I'm sorry. You must think I'm crazy. Where are we going for dinner?"

"Morton's steakhouse in Nashville. Ever been?"

"I have, and I love it."

"They deal with a lot of celebrities and politicians. They know how to be discreet, and they'll have a private room where we can be alone and talk."

The limo dropped us ten feet from the front door, and we were immediately surrounded and ushered into the restaurant by a small group of people, all of whom seemed to know exactly what the others were doing, as though the entire procession was choreographed. We were seated in a private room in less than two minutes, and in less than three minutes a waiter was handing me a bottle of wine. I looked at it, looked at him, and nodded. He opened it and set the cork on the table. I waved my hand to let him know I wasn't interested in the cork, and he poured a small amount of wine into a glass and handed it to me. I sniffed it first, took a small sip, and nodded again. He filled Lana's glass, then finished filling mine. I disliked upper-crust rituals, but I was not entirely without culture.

We ordered our meals a little while later, after the wine had had a chance to settle in and take effect. The service staff was attentive but not intrusive. They were there immediately if either Lana or I needed anything, but they didn't hover over the table. It was a perfect place to talk.

"I need to ask you about the night Kasey was killed, Lana," I said.

"I know."

"Tell me about it."

"There isn't much to tell, really. Where do you want me to start?"

"Wherever you think you need to start."

"All right. Well…Bennett drove me to the show around seven, and since Paul was supposed to be there, I told Bennett to go on home, that I would ride with Paul to the after-party and then ride home with him."

"So Paul and his driver, David, arrived at the show separately from you?"

"That's right. Paul came straight from the office. Paul is always at the office."

"And then the two of you rode to the after-party together?"

"No. I rode with Cameron Jones."

"The singer?"

"Right. He's another of Paul's artists."

"Why didn't you ride with Paul?"

"We were having a bit of a spat."

"Would you care to elaborate?"

"It was nothing, really. I'd had just a touch too much to drink, and then Paul and Kasey got into some kind of argument and she threw a glass of tea in his face, which made him look ridiculous. And then—"

I held up my hand. "Wait," I said. "Stop for just a second. Did you just say Paul and Kasey had some kind of argument that ended with her throwing a glass of tea in his face?"

"That's what I said."

"What were they arguing about?"

"Kasey surprised everyone by doing a song she wasn't supposed to do. She was supposed to perform this new song they're going to release for the summer called 'Party Girl.' The band, the orchestra, everybody had the music and was ready to go. The host even announced it to the audience. But when Kasey got up to the microphone, she told the audience there had been a slight change in plans. She had her guitar with her, and she sang a bluesy ballad she'd written called 'Blood Red Sun.' She nailed it, too. I was watching from the wings, and she sang and played that song for everything it was worth. The audience loved it as much as I did. They stood up and clapped and yelled when she was finished.

"But Paul was angry, and so were the show's producers, the director, the musicians, the tech people. They thought it was incredibly unprofessional for her to go off script like that, and it was. She shouldn't have done it. So a little while after she came off stage, she was standing in the wings with a glass of tea in her hand, and Paul walked up to her and you could tell it was getting pretty heated and then all of a sudden, *whoosh*, Kasey just tossed that tea right into his face and stalked off. Paul went to the restroom and cleaned himself up as best he could, but that kind of took the fun out of the evening, if you know what I mean."

"And what happened after that?"

"We all went to the after-party, and it was kind of subdued. I rode with Cameron because I was drunk and mad at Paul for not smacking Kasey upside her head or spitting in her face after she embarrassed him like that, and then at the after-party I started giving Paul a hard time for not standing up for himself after she doused him. Kasey and Paul hadn't said a word to each other, either, and then the next thing I knew I was saying a couple things I shouldn't have said to Kasey, and then she was gone. Then Paul says I started messing around with Cameron underneath the table—which I deny and don't remember at all—so Paul called Bennett to come and get me around one in the morning. I think Paul stayed on until around two, and then he went over to the hotel. He told me he went to Kasey's room to try to patch things up, but she wound up saying something that made him so angry he slapped her."

"What did she say?"

"I don't know. He wouldn't tell me. It must have been bad, though, because Paul and I have been married for fifteen years, and I've said some mean things to him and he hasn't ever once even given me the notion that he might slap me. Paul's a big sissy when it comes to physical confrontation. He'll take every last dime you have, but he'll make you feel good while he's doing it. He doesn't have a violent bone in his body."

"Did he say what happened after he slapped her?"

"He said he couldn't believe he'd done it. He said Kasey went straight to the bathroom and locked the door, so he left."

"Where did he go?"

"He came home. Called a cab and had the guy drive him all the way to Franklin."

"Do you know what time he got home?"

"I was passed out. He said he got home around three, and I don't have a reason not to believe him."

"Okay," I said, "you've explained the piece of skin they found wedged between Kasey Cartwright's teeth and the bruising, but what about the strangling? Any ideas?"

"Somebody else killed her, and they're letting him take the fall."

I thought about what I'd told Jack and Charlie earlier. The SODDI defense. Some Other Dude Done It. It looked like that was where we were headed.

"Any idea who that might be?" I asked.

"One of the usual suspects, I guess. A competitor in the record business. Could be a disgruntled artist who thinks Paul screwed him or her over. Maybe some jealous boyfriend of Kasey's or some deranged fan. Who knows? There are all kinds of possibilities."

"Have you and Paul talked about it?"

"A little."

"What did he say? He hasn't admitted anything to you, has he?"

"He said he has no idea who killed her."

"Do you believe him?"

She shrugged her shoulders. "I guess. I don't really have a reason not to."

I sat back and let out a deep breath. I must have had a concerned look on my face because Lana said, "What's wrong?"

"Nothing's wrong," I said. "I was just thinking we have a lot of ground to cover."

"Why don't you call Leon?" she said.

"Leon? Are you talking about Leon Bates?"

"Cute as a button, and I hear he's as good a lawman as there is. Y'all are friends, right? Why don't you bring him in to help?"

"He told me he knows you."

"He and his girlfriend stay in the same guesthouse you're staying in when they come to Nashville."

"Girlfriend? Are you talking about Erlene?"

"Erlene Barlowe. Sweet as she can be. Reminds me of my granny."

I smiled. Erlene Barlowe *was* as sweet as she could be on the exterior, but when threatened, she had the instincts of a pit viper.

"I can't believe you know them," I said. "Small world. But we can't use Leon. He has his hands full up in Washington County."

"Just a thought," Lana said.

I was drinking slowly, but Lana wasn't. She took large sips from the wine, and she took them frequently. She made two trips to the bathroom during the first hour we were at the restaurant. After her second trip, I started up the conversation again.

"Tell me about your marriage," I said, "and by that I mean your lives together. You and Paul. Tell me about you and Paul."

She took a long drink from her glass of wine and set it carefully on the table.

"We were quite the item back in our day. Downright scandalous. I was only eighteen, and Paul was twenty-nine. He was looking for new artists to build his record company, and I was looking for fame and fortune. I gave him what he wanted, and he gave me what I wanted."

"So it was good?"

"It was for a time, but the passion faded pretty quickly. We were both so busy. We were all over the country, all over the world even. We would go months without seeing each other."

"I haven't heard you use the word 'love' to describe the relationship, Lana."

"Love," she said with a sour look on her face. "People make such a big deal out of love. I don't even know what it really means, if it really exists."

"I do," I said.

"Then tell me, lawyer man, what does 'love' really mean?"

"Nah, I'm not here to talk about love according to Joe Dillard. I'm here to talk about you and Paul. Tell me why you quit the music business."

"Because I couldn't sing anymore. I lost my voice."

"That isn't what the press reported," I said.

"I know. They wanted another scandal, so they started reporting all kinds of crazy things. When I first started having problems with my voice, we made a public announcement that I was going to take a little time off— that I was exhausted—which was true. But since Paul and I are public figures, they can write pretty much anything they want to—there's nothing we can do about it. They started writing that we were breaking up, that Paul was seeing other women, that I was bisexual and was seeing a woman, all kinds of things. The lies generated so much publicity that my record sales skyrocketed. They actually benefitted us by lying about us. But the truth was that I'd abused my voice. I'd overused it and stretched my vocal cords to the point where several nodules developed on both of them. I went to the best surgeons in the world, and they all told me I was finished. Turned out they were right."

"You were saying you gave him what he wanted, and he gave you what you wanted," I said. "He wanted an up-and-coming artist, and you wanted fame and fortune. Are you still giving each other what you want?"

She held her hand up to refuse the dessert she'd ordered earlier and took another long pull of the wine.

"We have some stability, we're surrounded by luxury, we're as wealthy as we'd dreamed we could be," she said. "I don't have to do a damned thing if I don't want to, which is exactly the way I like it. Paul is still doing what he loves—he's just doing it with different people. So to answer your question, I guess we're still giving each other some of what we want, just not all of what we want. I actually see very little of Paul. We haven't had sex in more than a year, but that hasn't been because we aren't attracted to each other. We are, but Paul has had some problems with…well, you know…performance. It got to be embarrassing. It was so uncomfortable that we just stopped, you know? We didn't really talk about it. We just stopped."

"So you don't think he was having an affair with Kasey Cartwright?" I said.

Lana laughed loudly and nearly spit a mouthful of wine across the table.

"He isn't capable of having an affair," she said. "Unless he's just so repulsed by me that he can't get it up. Believe me…I've tried every trick I know, and I know a lot of them."

"Don't you get lonely?" I said, wishing I could grab the words and stuff them back into my mouth as soon as they escaped.

She gave me a look that could have melted a glacier and said, "Damned right I get lonely. Get a couple more glasses of this wine in me and you might just find out *how* lonely on the ride back to Franklin."

CHAPTER 11

By the time we got to Xanadu, Bennett the driver had to practically pour Lana out of the backseat, where she was taken into the arms of four people I hadn't seen earlier in the day and whisked off inside the house. Bennett dropped me near the front door of the guesthouse, which was a quarter mile from the main house. It was at least fifteen hundred square feet bigger than my home on Boone Lake but less than a quarter of the size of Milius's mansion. The sky was dark, the temperature freezing, and the wind howling as I got out of the car. Bennett made no effort to get out and open the door for me, and for that I was grateful because having people tend to my every need or whim embarrassed me. The holiday decorations had been turned off for the night, and in the cold darkness, Xanadu seemed as foreboding as an inner-city ghetto. As I made my way up the walk with the sound of Bennett's car fading behind me, an outside light came on, and the front door opened. A sixty-something man, dark-eyed, gray-haired and slim, smiled at me and half bowed as I walked into the house.

"Good evening, Mr. Dillard," he said.

"Good evening."

"I am Rafael Martinez. I will be at your service during your stay with us. May I take your coat?"

I stopped and looked at him for a long minute.

"Is something wrong, sir?" he said.

"Do you live here?" I asked. "I mean here in this house? Because I was here for a couple hours earlier today and you weren't here."

"No, sir. I have a place of my own a few miles away. When you were here earlier, I had not yet been informed by Mr. Payne that I was to be your personal assistant during your stay. Mr. Payne has been away on holiday vacation, and all of this with Mr. Milius has happened very quickly. We've all been shocked and caught off guard. I apologize for not having been here to assist you prior to your evening out with Mrs. Milius."

"I didn't need any assistance. Do you realize it's after midnight…uh…what did you say your name is?"

"Rafael."

"Do you realize it's after midnight, Rafael?"

"Yes, sir."

"Do you have a family?"

"I do. A wife and three children. The children have grown up and moved out of the house. The wife, unfortunately, remains both a child and at home."

"I appreciate you being here, Rafael, and I apologize in advance for what I'm about to say, but I'd really prefer that you leave and go home. I've never had a servant or a butler or an assistant or anything even close, and I have to tell you, it makes me uncomfortable. I don't mean to offend you. I'm sure you're a nice man, and I'm sure you're very good at what you do. It's just that I've been pretty much self-sufficient all my life, and I'd just as soon keep it that way."

"I apologize as well," Rafael said, "but I cannot go home. I cannot do as you ask. I would be fired first thing in the morning, and I don't want to be fired."

"All I'm going to do is go to bed," I said. "I'll wake up in the morning, take a shower, and get ready for the day. What can you possibly do for me?"

"Anything you want that isn't illegal or unseemly. I can turn your bed down, get you a beverage—a glass of warm milk or a drink from the bar. A glass of wine. I can get you a fine cigar. I can run you a hot bath, prepare a snack or a meal or run out and pick up take-out from anywhere that is still open. I can sit and visit with you—I can discuss a wide variety of topics intelligently—or I can simply go to my room and leave you to yourself. It's up to you. I cannot, however, go home and leave you here alone."

I shook my head, which was beginning to throb slightly.

"All right," I said. "Do you have any aspirin around? I feel a headache coming on."

"Certainly. What would you like to drink?'

"Water."

"Bottled or tap?"

"Tap is fine."

"Ice?"

"No, thanks."

He reached toward me. "Your coat, please?"

I took my coat off and handed it to him.

"It will be in the closet in your room near the bed," he said. "Will you be in the den?"

"Since you're going to stay anyway, I'd like to talk to you for a little while, if that's okay with you," I said.

"Certainly, sir."

I went into the den—a room with a twenty-foot ceiling—which featured a floor-to-ceiling, stone fireplace and a flat-screen television that was at least seventy inches across. I sat down on a plush, black leather couch. It had been a long day and I was exhausted, but there was something about Rafael that made me want to speak with him. It was difficult to put into words, but I'd been forced to deal with so many people in my life who had personal agendas or motives to deceive that I sometimes found myself drawn to people who gave me the sense that were simply honest, and Rafael gave me that sense. I was aware that I could be completely wrong about the assessment, but I decided to take a chance.

Rafael walked in a few minutes later carrying a glass of water in one hand and three aspirin in a small paper cup in the other. He handed them to me. I thanked him and motioned for him to sit in an overstuffed chair a few feet away.

"You said earlier that Mr. Payne sent you here to the house," I said.

"Yes, sir."

"Who is Mr. Payne?"

"Oliver Payne. He is Mr. and Mrs. Milius's estate manager."

"Estate manager? What's that?"

"He manages the household affairs, the grounds, the aircraft and runway, the horses, pretty much everything. He hires and manages the staff, and by 'the staff' I mean the housekeepers and the cooks and the servers and the people who do the laundry and the drivers and the flight attendant and pilot. All of those things."

"So he's a glorified butler or major domo," I said.

"Mr. Payne is a highly educated man," Rafael said. "He has an MBA from one of the Ivy League schools and an undergraduate degree in finance and accounting. Mr. Milius has other real estate—a home in Palm Beach and another in Connecticut—and Mr. Payne manages those properties as well. My understanding is that he and Mr. Milius—and Mrs. Milius, of course—develop a budget each year and then Mr. Payne operates the properties within the confines of the budget. I've heard Mr. Payne describe it as a corporate approach to personal asset management. If Mr. Payne comes in under budget, the staff gets a bonus, which encourages all of us not to be wasteful."

I thought about the irony of that comment for a moment. Paul and Lana Milius consumed more in terms of energy in one day than my entire family did in a month. They were hardly frugal.

"So is Mr. Payne well paid?" I said.

"I don't know the exact figure, but yes, I suspect he is well paid. I've heard Mrs. Milius complain about it on a couple occasions when she was a bit tipsy."

"What about you and the rest of the staff? Slave wages or fair wages?"

"Very fair," Rafael said. "Everyone who works for Mr. Milius receives a good salary and full benefits. I make more than six figures and have health coverage and an IRA, for instance. I get three weeks of paid vacation each year."

"How many people work for Mr. Milius here at the estate?"

"It varies. People come and go, but I would guess the average is fifteen to sixteen."

"Any one of those fifteen or sixteen have a problem with Mr. Milius? A serious problem? Maybe a former employee?"

"Not that I know of. Mr. Milius actually has very little contact with the staff outside, say, meals he eats here on the weekends. During the week, he leaves early in the morning and returns late at night, and he is often gone on the weekends. He takes most of his meals with business associates. So as far as anyone having a problem with him to the extent that they would do something to harm him or do something like killing Kasey Cartwright and making it appear that Mr. Milius did it, which is what you seem to be implying, well, I think those things would be rather unlikely."

A thought struck me and I sat up.

"Rafael, tell me something," I said. "You've been assigned to be my personal assistant, and I'm only here for a couple days. Lana has a personal assistant, Lisa Trent. I met her as soon as I got here this morning. But nobody has mentioned Paul having a personal assistant. I've met his driver, David, but David doesn't strike me as personal-assistant material. He's a little rough around the edges. Am I missing something?"

Up until that moment, Rafael had been relaxed and friendly, but as soon as I asked about the personal assistant, his face tightened and he stood.

"If there is nothing else, then, I suppose I will see you in the morning," he said.

"Okay," I said.

"Good night, Mr. Dillard," Rafael said, and he turned and walked out of the room.

CHAPTER 12

A s it turned out, there were fifteen people working for Paul and Lana at the estate: Lana's personal assistant, Lisa; the two drivers, David and Bennett; Oliver Payne, the estate manager, who was away on vacation and wouldn't return for two and a half weeks; Rafael, who was a sort of utility servant and second-in-command beneath Payne; Michael, the grumpy chef; three assistant chefs; four housekeepers and two groundskeepers that doubled as handymen. There was also a fairly extensive list of outside contractors who came to the house when they were needed and another group of people who took care of the horses, but I decided not to interview them unless something came up that indicated I really needed to.

I had planned to interview the employees at the guesthouse, but early on the morning after my conversation with Rafael, I found a disturbing note pinned to the inside pocket of my jacket when I was putting it on. Rafael had insisted on laying out my clothes for the day, so he must have left the note. It said, in a slanted scrawl, "Be careful. There are cameras and microphones all over the house." Once I read that, I decided to use Charlie Story's office for the interviews and called Lana immediately.

"I know I said I'd like to interview everyone at the guesthouse," I said when she answered in a thick, hungover voice, "but I've decided to do it at the office I'll be using in Nashville. It's more professional, and I think the employees will be more willing to be open with me if the interviews are done at a neutral location."

"What? You want to go all the way to Nashville?" she said.

"It isn't far. You can send them individually or in groups, however you want to do it. Just make sure I get at least one per hour for the next two days. Have the first one there at nine o'clock."

She started to protest, but I told her I had another call and cut her off.

During the first day, I learned that all the employees were hired through a staffing agency in Nashville that catered to the wealthy. I learned that all of them were thoroughly vetted before they were hired. I was also astounded at the salaries. The housekeepers and the drivers made $75,000 a year, as did the groundskeepers. The chefs made closer to $100,000, and Michael made $120,000. As for Paul Milius, not a single one of the employees had a bad word to say about him, and none of them said they had ever seen him display anger, let alone engage in any sort of violent behavior. Lana, they said, was extremely intelligent, somewhat aloof, and frequently intoxicated. Not much of a surprise there.

Around ten o'clock in the morning on the second day, Michael Pillston, the chef, walked in. He was wearing black trousers and loafers and a powder-blue pullover shirt.

"When you said, 'Welcome to Xanadu, Mr. Dillard. I hope it isn't your downfall,' what did you mean?" I said after we exchanged greetings and he got settled in.

"Nothing, really. I was just being facetious."

"Have you been with Paul and Lana for a long time?"

"Six and a half years."

"So you know them pretty well?"

"Not really. I'm a slave. They're the masters. How well does one really get to know his master?"

"But you live in the house, don't you?" I asked.

"I do. I live there because Lana wants a cook at her beck and call twenty-four hours a day, seven days a week. Not that she eats all that much. But if she wants something, she wants it immediately, and she wants it done right. I do it right."

"What about Paul? Is he demanding?"

"I rarely see him, so I suppose the answer is no."

"You seem like a fairly straightforward person to me," I said, "so I'm just going to go ahead and ask you a direct question. Nobody else seems to want to talk about this, but maybe you will. What happened to Paul and Lana's personal assistants?"

"Lana has a personal assistant."

"Right, but she's only been around for a month. Her assistant prior to that was her first cousin, a woman named Tilly Hart. She's a year younger than Lana, and they grew up together in McNairy County. She was Lana's assistant for fifteen years. Paul's assistant was a thirty-year-old named Alex Pappas. He was around for three years before he left, apparently after stealing a bunch of money by using a credit card Paul had given him. They both fell off the face of the earth on Thanksgiving and haven't been heard from since. I've been able to get that much, but it's been like pulling teeth."

Michael folded his arms and tilted his head. "You asked me what happened to them," he said. "The answer is I have no idea."

"What do you think might have happened to them?"

"I think perhaps they ran away together."

"And why would they do that?"

"Why does anyone run away? My guess is that something, or someone, scared them."

"Paul?"

"Probably not."

"Lana?"

"That would be a more reasonable conclusion."

"Why?"

"Because Lana can be unstable. She's bitter and she drinks too much. I think she may be bipolar, even psychotic sometimes. I think Lana may have attempted to leverage the feelings Alex and Tilly had developed for each other. I think she may have tried to force one or the other of them to do something they didn't want to do and maybe threatened the other in the process."

"You said she may have tried to force one or the other of them to do something they didn't want to do. What didn't they want to do?"

"Something terrible, I would think."

"Something violent?"

"Neither of them would ever engage in violence, but she might have forced them to facilitate an act of violence."

"Facilitate? Are you telling me that Kasey Cartwright might have been killed by a contractor? Is that what you're telling me? And that Lana Raines forced either Tilly or Alex or both to help set it up?"

"I didn't say any of those things," Michael said.

"Do you have any direct knowledge of any of those things? Have you heard or seen anything?"

He looked at me strangely for several seconds. His eyes seemed like they were smiling.

"I will not testify," he said. "My official answers to those questions are no and no."

"What are your unofficial answers?"

"I like living in that house, Mr. Dillard. I'm overpaid and underworked. Lana drinks most of her meals, and Paul rarely eats at home. They hardly ever entertain, and when they do, they hire caterers. The surroundings are luxurious, and the perks are generous. I'd be a fool to throw it away."

"I'd appreciate it if you'd stop being cavalier, Michael," I said. "Have you heard or seen anything that would be relevant to the guilt or innocence of Paul Milius?"

Michael looked to my right and nodded toward a small stack of legal pads.

"May I?" he said.

"Of course."

He picked up a legal pad and a pen that was lying next to it. Then he wrote something on the pad and slid it toward me. It said, "Carl Browning, Attorney at Law." Michael then pulled a set of keys from his pocket and pointed at one them. He pointed to the paper, then to the key, to the paper, to the key.

"Have a nice day, Mr. Dillard," he said, and he got up and started toward the door.

"Wait, please," I said, and he stopped.

"Were you close to Alex or Tilly?" I asked.

"Tilly and I had become close," he said. "Alex and Tilly started dating each other nearly a year ago and had fallen head over heels in love. And then one day they were here, and the next day they were gone. They didn't say a word to anyone. They apparently took only what they could fit in a suitcase."

"Why didn't anyone call the police, especially since they supposedly stole a bunch of money?"

"Good question. You should ask Lana and Paul about that."

"I will. Please give some thought to telling me everything you know and testifying in court if the need arises," I said.

"I'll think about it," he said, "but I doubt very seriously that I'll change my mind."

"Why?" I said. "If you know the truth, why would you not want it to come out?"

"That's simple, Mr. Dillard. I have no desire to wind up like young Kasey." And then he whispered, "Check out the lawyer."

CHAPTER 13

afael came in near the end of the second day, the next-to-last person I interviewed. He seemed nervous as he sat in a chair across from me. He kept tapping his index fingers together and involuntarily pursing his lips. He was casually dressed in a tan button-down and khaki pants and was perfectly groomed. He hadn't been at the house the previous evening when I arrived and hadn't showed up later that night.

"I thought you were supposed to be my personal servant during my visit," I said to him.

"Plans change sometimes," he said.

"Care to elaborate?"

"My wife became ill. I had to take her to the emergency room."

"I'm sorry to hear that. Is she all right?"

"Yes, unfortunately."

I smiled and tapped the pen I was holding on the desk. "You and your wife have grown apart over the years?" I asked.

"She whines too much," Rafael said. "Nothing is ever satisfactory. We don't have enough money. The house is too small. The yard isn't mowed properly. The flower garden isn't pretty enough. The vegetable garden isn't yielding what it should. The cat sheds."

"Like I said, I'm sorry to hear it. Thank you for the note, by the way."

"Note? What note?"

"Doesn't matter, but thanks just the same."

"What about you, Mr. Dillard? Are you married?"

"I am."

"How long?"

"Two and a half decades, give or take a few months."

"And are you still in love?"

"Desperately, but I didn't ask you here to talk about my personal life. I need to talk about *your* life, and especially what you know about Lana and Paul Milius."

"I know they are two people who, like my wife and me, have grown apart," Rafael said. "But unlike my wife and me, there is an element of danger around the house, especially where Mrs. Milius is concerned. I would advise you to be extremely careful in your dealings with her."

"You're not the first person to tell me that," I said. "What can you tell me about Mr. Milius?"

"Very little. He was hardly ever around. There were a lot of rumors, though."

"What kind of rumors?"

"He apparently enjoyed sampling the housekeepers from time to time."

"Sampling? Are you talking about having sex with them? I've been told he has problems with…with…erectile dysfunction."

Rafael laughed aloud. "Really? Someone told you Mr. Milius is impotent?"

I nodded.

"You have been lied to, Mr. Dillard. I'm sure you'll discover as you get into the case that Mr. Milius is anything but impotent. As a matter of fact, he should probably be in therapy for sex addiction."

"How do you know that?"

Rafael looked around the room slowly, as though he was searching for recording devices. He crossed his arms and began rubbing his hands up and down.

"Relax," I said. "Nothing you say will leave this room."

"I will not testify," he said. "If you try to call me to testify, I'll disappear, just like Alex did."

"Were you and Alex friends?"

"We were. That's how I know about Mr. Milius."

"How close?"

"He was very busy, as was I, but we managed to spend some time together. We had many things in common. We're both liberals. We both spoke fluent Spanish, played classical guitar, and we both loved Latin beers and soccer. Alex was the son of a Greek father and an Ecuadoran mother. I am Chilean. He visited my home several times. Over the past year, Tilly came with him. They were a beautiful couple, so young and so vibrant together. They reminded me of my wife and me in happier times."

"Do you know what happened to them?"

"To the best of my knowledge, they became enmeshed in a situation that threatened their lives, so they left."

"Can you tell me about the situation? What did it involve?"

"Alex wouldn't be specific. He just said he was sorry but they had to leave, and he said I shouldn't believe anything Lana said about him or Tilly after they were gone. And I don't. Alex was not a thief, and I don't believe Tilly was, either."

"Does Alex have money? Or Tilly? Are either of them wealthy?"

"Alex was frugal and I know he was paid quite well, so I would guess that he has accumulated some money. From what he said, I gathered that his family is quite wealthy. As for Tilly, I can't really say."

"Can you give me any sort of timeline?"

"I noticed a change in Alex maybe the second week of November. It happened very, very quickly. He was short with me, distracted, and seemed terribly fidgety. He virtually stopped answering his phone, and he wouldn't return my phone calls if I left him a message. Then, the night before Thanksgiving, he showed up at my house unannounced and told me he was leaving. He wasn't there long, and he was very emotional. He asked me not to say anything to anyone and I promised him I wouldn't, and then two days later, the word began to spread through the house that he and Tilly were gone. Then a day or two after that, the rumor started spreading that Alex had spent a huge amount of money using a credit card that belonged to Mr. Milius."

"But nobody called the police," I said.

"Exactly."

"Then just a couple weeks after that the young country singer was killed and the police started coming around and rumors started flying that Mr. Milius was involved. Then he was arrested, and now here we are."

"So you believe Alex and Tilly's disappearance is connected to Kasey Cartwright's murder."

"It would just be too much of a coincidence for them not to be connected."

"Have you heard anything from Alex since he left?"

"Not a word," Rafael said, "and frankly, I don't expect to hear anything from him. Not for a long, long time, if ever."

"Where do you think they went?"

"I really have no idea. They could be hiding in plain sight somewhere in Tennessee, or maybe they went to a big city like New York or Los Angeles. Or maybe they left the country."

"Ecuador, maybe?"

"Or any other Spanish-speaking country. Take a look at a map of the world, Mr. Dillard. There are a lot of them. They could be anywhere."

CHAPTER 14

"I have bad news and terrible news," the lawyer said. "Which do you want first?"

They were walking through Centennial Park as a gentle snow fell. Lana had told her driver to drop her off at the entrance of the First Fifth Bank downtown and instructed him to wait in the parking lot until she called. She had immediately called a cab and ridden to Centennial Park where she met Carl Browning. It was ten o'clock in the morning, classes had not yet resumed at nearby Vanderbilt, and the park was almost empty.

"I'm beginning to loathe you," Lana said, her breath misting in the cold air. "It seems like every time you contact me, something else has gone wrong."

"You didn't answer the question," Browning said. "Bad or terrible first?"

"Stop playing childish games and say what you have to say," Lana said harshly.

"The money's gone," Browning said. "It's taken me all this time—and almost $100,000 in bribe money—to get around the Channel Islands secrecy laws and get a bead on the bank account Alex set up. I mean, he did it exactly how we wanted it done. There's no way it could ever be traced back to any of us, but all the money he deposited has been transferred out of the account. The first half of it went out on the tenth of November, and it went to an account controlled by the company we hired to do this job. I spoke with our contact that day to confirm."

"And the rest of it?" Lana said.

"It apparently went to a bank in the Cayman Islands," Browning said.

"When?"

"The day before Thanksgiving."

"Into an account controlled by whom?"

"I don't know. What I do know is that it wasn't controlled by the company we hired, and that's where the terrible news comes in."

"What are you talking about, Carl?" Lana said. "You're not making any sense."

"I got a message yesterday afternoon from our contact. They want the rest of the money. They want the full contract price."

Lana stopped and faced him, her cheeks flush with anger.

"What do you mean, the full contract price?" she hissed. "They only did half the job! There were supposed to be two bodies in that hotel room. Two! That's what we were supposed to be paying them for. They didn't live up to their end."

"That isn't how they see it," Browning said. "Their spin is that they were told to be at a certain place at a certain time and that the targets would be there. We told them they'd be in bed together, that it would be easy. Instead, Paul left, didn't come back, and they were only able to get to Kasey. They say they're not responsible for bad intelligence, and they want the other half of the money."

"I hope you told them to go screw themselves," Lana said as they continued walking.

"These aren't exactly the kind of people you say that to, Lana."

"Then I suggest you start spreading some money around in the Caymans and find out where the other half is."

"I could do that, but my guess is that the money went from the Caymans to the Seychelles or to Samoa, maybe through Switzerland, maybe to some obscure place like Brunei. We might never find out where it went, and even if we do, we'll probably never be able to get our hands on it."

"So what you're telling me is that some little olive picker who probably didn't know shit from Shinola about international finance three months ago and a froo-froo-haired redneck girl from McNairy County have out-smarted you? Is that what you're telling me, Carl?"

"They didn't out*smart* me, Lana. They just…they just—"

"*Stole two and a half million dollars of my money!*"

The lawyer dropped his head. There was nothing he could say.

CHAPTER 15

ana showed up in the guesthouse at eight o'clock, just as I was zipping up my suitcase to leave for home. Rafael had been there when I arrived, but he'd already left. He'd seemed genuinely disappointed that I refused to allow him to help me pack. Lana was wearing jeans and a pink blouse and seemed sober. I could hear the jet taxiing onto the runway outside.

"Just wanted to say bye," Lana said.

"That's nice of you. I appreciate the hospitality."

"How did your interviews go?" she asked.

"Went good."

"Did you learn anything I need to know about?"

"Nothing earth-shattering," I said as I pulled my suitcase off the bed, "but there is one thing I'd like to ask you about before I go."

"What's that?"

"Why did you tell me Paul is impotent?"

She seemed startled by the question at first but quickly regained her composure.

"I was just kidding," she said.

"Seems like a strange thing to joke about."

"I have to laugh about it, Mr. Dillard...excuse me, Joe. If I didn't, I'd spend a lot of time crying."

"So he's been unfaithful?"

"Unfaithful would be an understatement."

"Why don't you divorce him?"

"And run the risk of losing all this? How silly would that be? We have an open marriage now. He does what he wants, and I do what I want."

"So you don't mind that your husband has sex with other women," I said.

"I'd be dishonest if I said it doesn't bother me sometimes, or at least it used to," she said, "but I've learned to deal with it. It's like I told you at the restaurant. I don't much believe in love anymore. I've grown past all that."

"That's too bad," I said. "Thank you again for the jet and the house and the meal the other night. I'll see you again soon."

"Keep something in mind for me, would you?" Lana said.

"What's that?"

"Paul being a philanderer doesn't make him a murderer."

"That's very understanding of you, Lana. Oh, just one more thing. Carl Browning? Is he your attorney?"

"Carl represents me, yes. He handles all my business affairs."

"Good lawyer?"

"Yes, very good."

"Good guy?"

"Why do you ask?"

"No big deal. Somebody mentioned him. Do you spend a lot of time with Carl? And by that I mean is he maybe a boyfriend? You just said Paul does what he wants, and you do what you want. Is Carl one of the things you want?"

"Carl and I are strictly business," Lana said.

"Okay, then. Thanks again for everything."

"Have a nice flight," Lana said, smiling her biggest smile, and I walked out and got into the waiting car.

CHAPTER 16

arrived back home at around nine o'clock at night after spending two and a half days in Nashville. It was cold and dark, but Caroline was standing under a street-light, waiting for me near the private charter gate in back of the airport. When I got close and could see her long hair flowing and her dark eyes shining, it was like I was seeing her for the very first time. I walked through the gate, lifted her off the ground in a bear hug, and kissed her.

"I missed you," I said.

"I missed you, too. I had to turn off the office line. It wouldn't stop ringing."

"Press?" I asked, and she nodded.

I loaded my bag into the trunk of her car and got into the passenger seat. I gave her a brief outline of the Life of Milius at the Mansion, but she seemed distracted.

"What's wrong?" I said after we'd driven a couple of miles.

"I'm almost afraid to tell you," she said.

"Why?"

"Because I know you, and I know your first reaction is going to be anger. Please try to take this calmly."

"What did Sarah do?" I said.

"Promise you won't get mad."

"I promise. Well, I semi-promise. It depends."

"It isn't your sister. It's your son-in-law. Randy got arrested for DUI."

"Shit," I said, feeling my blood pressure rise.

"I know."

"When?"

"Last night."

"Last night? He got arrested for DUI on a freaking *Tuesday*? Who gets arrested for DUI on a *Tuesday*?"

"Joe, you semi-promised."

"I know, but what the...? What the...? What time was it?"

"Around eleven."

"Where was he? What was he doing?"

"He apparently went to the store and had an accident. The car ran off the road into a ditch. He said he fell asleep."

"Is he still on the pills?"

"I don't know. It appears that way."

Randy had been in yet another accident six months earlier, although that one wasn't his fault. He had been T-boned on his way to school by a woman who thought it was more important to be texting than paying attention to what she was doing and had blown through a stop sign. The wreck had broken his femur and fractured several of his ribs and two vertebrae, and while there was never any real concern that he might die, he had been in considerable pain for several weeks. He'd taken opiates to mask the pain, and before he knew it, he was addicted. He also apparently enjoyed the feeling he got when he mixed the opiates with alcohol, because Lilly had mentioned to Caroline and me that he'd been drinking far more than he ever had before. We'd all sat down and had what I thought was a productive discussion with Randy about it. I even asked Sarah—an expert on addiction and the problems it can cause—to talk to him, and she had, but our words had obviously not had the desired effect.

"Have they suspended him from school?" I asked. Randy was in his third year of medical school.

"I don't think he's told them yet."

"What do you know about it? Do you know what his blood alcohol content was?"

"All I know is that he fell asleep and wrecked. When he wrecked, he hit his head on the steering wheel, and it knocked him out. He was unconscious when the police officer got there. The officer apparently smelled alcohol on him. He got the results of the tox screen from the hospital, and when they released Randy the next morning, the officer was waiting with a warrant. They took him to jail and Lilly bailed him out."

"Where was Lilly while he was driving off to the store drunk?"

"She was in bed, Joe. She had no idea he was leaving."

I shook my head and took an involuntary deep breath. "This isn't good," I said. "This could screw up his entire career. This could screw up their lives."

"I know," Caroline said. "Lilly was beside herself until I talked to her and calmed her down. I told her exactly what she needed to hear."

"What was that?"

"I told her that her father would be home soon, and he'd take care of it. You have to fix this, Joe. This is family. You have to get him out of this."

CHAPTER 17

I met Randy for lunch the next morning at a place called Café One Eleven in Johnson City. I'd asked him to meet me at eleven o'clock so we could talk privately before the place filled up. We sat at a table in the back of the restaurant and ordered our meals. Randy was a good-looking kid, solidly built with sandy-brown hair and bright, blue eyes. He'd always been a good husband and a good father, and as far as I knew, he was an excellent medical student. He was in the middle of his third year and said he hoped to graduate summa cum laude. We got along well, but I noticed his hands were trembling slightly when he took a sip of the water he'd ordered.

"So I hear you had an adventure while I was gone," I said to him.

"If you want to call it that," Randy said. He was looking at the tabletop, and there were small beads of sweat on his forehead.

"A DUI charge? On a Tuesday night? Third year in med school? What in the hell were you thinking?"

"Don't start," he said. "The last thing I need right now is you ragging on me."

"I think you're wrong about that. The last thing you need is a DUI conviction. They'll toss you out of school for that, won't they?"

"They could. I mean, I've seen them do it, but I'm not planning on pleading guilty, and I'm not planning on being found guilty. I'll get out of this clean."

"Really?" I said. "Exactly how are you planning to do that?"

"I'm going to hire this lawyer out of Knoxville named Charles Freeze. Ever heard of him?"

I nodded. Charlie Freeze was probably the best DUI defense lawyer in the state of Tennessee. I'd talked to him several times over the years. He'd written a treatise on DUI defense that I'd read half a dozen times, and he was on the board of directors of the Tennessee Trial Lawyers Association. He was also one of the most expensive DUI lawyers in the Southeastern United States. DUI was a misdemeanor, but I'd heard Charlie charged in excess of $15,000 to take on a case.

"Why are you hiring Charlie Freeze when I'm perfectly willing to handle this for you for free?" I said.

"I'm sorry, Joe. I don't mean to hurt your feelings or anything, but I just think you're maybe a little too close. I'm afraid your relationship with Lilly and me might cloud your judgment. I obviously need somebody that's good, but I also want it to be somebody who can deal with it at arm's length. No emotion involved in the decision-making process. Pure analytics, the same thing they teach us over at the med school."

"Have you talked to him?"

"I was in his office in Knoxville at seven thirty this morning. We talked for an hour and I drove back."

"How much is he going to charge you?"

"Seventeen five."

"What? Did you just say $17,500?"

"Yeah. He says if I can pay, he'll get me out of it."

"He made you a guarantee?"

"Not exactly a guarantee, but he said he can handle it. My blood alcohol level was point zero five, which is below the legal limit. I tested positive for opioids, but it was just a tox screen and they didn't quantify the amount of opioids I had in my system. Since I was unconscious, they didn't talk to me at the scene, and they don't have any kind of field sobriety tests on video. They won't be able to prove intoxication. At least that's what he says."

The waitress brought our lunches, and I waited for her to get out of earshot before I resumed the conversation.

"So $17,500," I said. "Do you have that kind of money?"

Randy wiped his mouth with a napkin and took a drink from his water.

"I was kind of hoping you might help us out with that," he said. "Since you just got this new case and everything I was hoping you might loan me the money. I'm going to be a doctor in a couple years. It's not like I won't be able to pay you back."

"You're not going to be a doctor if you don't clean up your act," I said.

"Please, Joe," he said. "I'll take care of that end of it. I promise. Can you help me out with Freeze?"

I leaned forward on my elbows and sat there looking at him. The image that immediately came into my mind was of Lilly saying, "Please, Daddy, he's trying so hard. Everybody makes mistakes." I reached down and picked up a forkful of shrimp and rice and shoved it into my mouth.

"Sure," I said after I swallowed. "You want me to write the check to you or to Freeze?"

* * *

After I left Randy, I had this nagging sense that he wasn't being completely honest with me. He'd had difficulty maintaining eye contact during lunch, and he'd seemed distracted and irritable. I supposed those things could have been perfectly natural under the circumstances, but I felt as though he was hiding something. I decided to take a little side trip down to Jonesborough to the clerk's office of the General Sessions Court, which was where all the misdemeanor criminal cases in the county were filed. The records were open to public inspection, and I knew there would be a copy of Randy's arrest warrant and a copy of the sworn affidavit the police officer filed in support of the warrant. I walked into the justice center—the ugly, expensive architectural disaster that had replaced the old but perfectly serviceable courthouse several years earlier—a little after twelve thirty, exchanged greetings with the deputies manning the security checkpoints, and made my way down the hall to the clerk's office. An attractive, gray-haired woman named Lynn Weber whom I'd known for a couple decades walked up and said hello. I asked her for a copy of the warrant and affidavit. She handed them to me in just a couple minutes, and I walked back out to the hall and sat down on a wooden bench.

As soon as I started reading, I felt the pulsing in my temples that told me my blood pressure was rising. It became obvious very quickly why Randy didn't want me to handle the case and why he had traveled all the way to Knoxville to hire a lawyer. The fact that he had asked me to loan him the money to pay the lawyer made me even angrier.

The officer who wrote the affidavit, a Johnson City patrol officer named Jon Grady, said he was notified by an emergency dispatcher of an accident with injuries at approximately 11:03 p.m. on Tuesday night. When Officer Grady arrived, he was met by a young woman who identified herself as Tiffany Hill. Miss Hill told the officer that the driver of the vehicle, Randy Lowe, had just picked her up from her apartment and that they were "just talking and riding around." Miss Hill said a car coming toward them in the opposite lane crossed the centerline and forced them off the road. Randy's car went through a roadside ditch and hit a small tree. Miss Hill was uninjured, but Randy's head hit the steering wheel and he was knocked unconscious. He regained consciousness after the emergency medical people arrived, but they took him directly to the emergency room.

Officer Grady tried to talk with him at the emergency room, but Randy refused. Grady said he smelled alcohol on Randy when he got close to him and said there was an empty, thirty-two-ounce beer bottle in plain view on the floorboard of the backseat of Randy's car. Officer Grady said he asked Miss Hill whether Randy had been drinking, and she replied, "I don't know. Maybe. He didn't seem drunk."

Based on his observations at the accident scene, the odor of alcohol on Randy, and the empty beer bottle, Officer Grady applied for and was granted a search warrant for the results of Randy's blood toxicity screen that emergency rooms across the country give to nearly every patient that walks in the door. When he saw that Randy had opioids mixed with the .05 blood alcohol level, he got an arrest warrant.

Randy was probably right about one thing: Officer Grady didn't have much of a case. Without quantifying the opioids, it would be extremely difficult to prove beyond a reasonable doubt that Randy was operating the vehicle while under the influence.

But the greater issue for me was this: who in the hell was Tiffany Hill, and what was she doing in my daughter's husband's car? I took my cell phone out of my pocket and dialed the number of an old friend.

CHAPTER 18

Kasey Cartwright lived—before someone killed her, of course—in an idyllic spot. A two-story, white farmhouse, perfectly maintained, sat on a small hill overlooking a pond, a barn, a large corral and pasture land that stretched to the horizon in every direction. Kasey had graduated from Daniel Boone High School in Gray—the same high school my kids attended—just months before her death, even though she was already a star in the country music industry. She hadn't been home-schooled, hadn't moved to Nashville. She had toured only in the summer. From everything I'd been able to gather, she'd wanted to stay as grounded and as close to home as she could for as long as she could.

Kasey had been raised by her grandparents, Mike and Sandra Cartwright, on a dairy farm near the Sulphur Springs community in Washington County. Kasey's parents had been killed by a woman who fell asleep at the wheel early one morning when Kasey and her brother, James, were both very young. Kasey's mother and father were both schoolteachers and were riding to work together when the woman hit them. They had just dropped Kasey and James off at a daycare center. The woman wasn't injured and wasn't charged with a crime.

It was simply a terrible, tragic accident that left two children orphaned.

I knocked on the farmhouse door around two o'clock, about two hours after I'd left Randy. The afternoon was cold and dreary. Caroline had arranged the visit while I was in Nashville and had told me that Sandra Cartwright was cordial and respectful on the phone, but I was anxious about how I would be received. I was, after all, defending the man accused of killing their grandchild.

Sandra Cartwright was a sturdy, handsome woman who looked to be in her late fifties. Her hair was long and gray and pulled neatly into a ponytail that traveled the length of her back. Her eyes were light blue and soft, her skin pale and gracefully aging. She shook my hand firmly and invited me into a clean, comfortable den that was dominated by a brick fireplace. A row of framed photographs were arranged across the mantle. I noticed Kasey smiling in two of them.

"Coffee?" she said.

"Thank you. Black."

I sat down on a couch while Sandra went into the kitchen. She returned with two cups of steaming coffee, set one down in front of me, and took a seat in a chair across from me.

"I'm sorry for your loss, Mrs. Cartwright," I said. "I really am."

She nodded slightly in response and said, "What can I do for you, Mr. Dillard?"

"I just want to talk about Kasey," I said. "I want to get a sense of what she was like, who she was."

"So you can defame her when the trial starts? Isn't that what defense lawyers do, try to blame the victim? Engage in character assassination?"

"No, Mrs. Cartwright. I have absolutely no intention of saying anything bad about your granddaughter at the trial. In fact, I give you my word. But I should tell you up front that I don't believe Paul Milius killed her. She was an up-and-coming star. She was making him a lot of money. He'd spent a lot of time and money and effort building her career over the past three years. It just doesn't make sense."

"The police obviously feel differently."

"Speaking of the police, have you talked to them?"

"We heard from them on the day they found Kasey's body in the hotel," she said. "An investigator from the Washington County Sheriff's Department came out and talked to Mike and me. He told us she'd been killed and asked a few questions and we gave him her diary and a cell phone we found – it wasn't the one she usually carried – but we didn't hear another word until Sheriff Bates called and told us they'd made an arrest in Nashville."

I had suspected as much. The police had zeroed in on Paul Milius immediately. Once he had admitted to them that he'd been in Kasey's room that night, they hadn't bothered to look any further. I could understand it to a point. At trial, they could put Paul at the hotel through his driver's testimony and through the statement they had taken from him. They had a DNA match between the piece of skin in Kasey's mouth and Paul. I was sure there would be a couple witnesses to testify about the little rift at the Artists of the Year show. Pennington Frye had mentioned something about an insurance policy during one of my brief conversations with him. If Paul took the witness stand at trial, he would have to admit under oath that he'd been in Kasey's room because he told the police as much during one of his ill-advised interviews. And it wouldn't be that difficult for the jury to make the leap from assault to murder. It wasn't an ironclad case, but I'd seen convictions on less evidence.

"Well, like I said, Mrs. Cartwright, I don't think Paul Milius did this," I said. "Besides the fact that Kasey was making him so much money, he seems genuine when he expresses his feelings of affection for her. I've interviewed his wife and all his household staff—there are fifteen of them—and they all speak highly of him. None of them has ever seen him act violently or heard him raise his voice."

"He slapped Kasey in the mouth, didn't he?" Mrs. Cartwright said.

I nodded. "He apparently did, and he won't tell me, or anyone else, why. He and Kasey had some kind of disagreement at the CMT show earlier in the evening, and Kasey threw a glass of tea on him—"

"She wasn't supposed to sing that song," Mrs. Cartwright said as a small smile crossed her lips. "I knew it as soon as she started singing. She felt very strongly about her music. She wanted to stay true to it, if you can understand that. She'd talked to me many times about how they wanted her to sing songs that had commercial appeal to young people, songs about smoking dope and drinking and partying around bonfires all night and having promiscuous sex. But that just wasn't Kasey. She wasn't like that at all. I'll bet that's what they were arguing about."

"You're probably right," I said, "but it doesn't seem like a reason to kill her. I simply can't come up with a reason why Paul Milius would have killed your granddaughter, and my experience when it comes to murder has been that the *why* is inseparable from the *who*. My job now is to find out who really killed her, and while I'm at it, to find out *why* she was killed. I think the police jumped to conclusions early on and maybe rushed things a little. I don't think they were as thorough as they might have been. And that's one of the reasons I'm here. If there's anything you can tell me about Kasey—or anything you can show me—that might help me find out why she was killed, then maybe I can figure out who did it. Did she have a boyfriend, Mrs. Cartwright?"

She shook her head, almost imperceptibly, and sighed.

"She dated a boy named Ricky Church for two years," she said. "What a mess that was."

"Ricky Church?" I said, writing the name down on a small pad I carried in my pocket. "Is he from here?"

"Lives about three miles up the road. Same age as Kasey, went to the same school. He's a musician, too, or at least he thinks he is. Plays the guitar, but I can't listen to it. Kasey liked his music, but I didn't."

"Why's that?"

"It was just so different," she said. "They let him play a song at a school concert in the spring, and I thought my head was going to explode. Loud guitars and all this electric synthesizer going on. I couldn't understand a word he sang. When Kasey made fun of him—which wasn't often and never when he was around—she called him Ricky Emo. He was just so melodramatic about everything."

"Was he violent?" I asked.

"Not toward Kasey, but I know he'd been in several fights at school."

"Drugs?"

"I wouldn't know about that."

I heard a noise outside, and Mrs. Carpenter got up from the chair she'd been sitting in and looked out the front window.

"Oh, my," she said. "Oh, no."

"What's wrong?" I asked, turning to look at her.

"My husband. He isn't supposed to…he won't like this—you being here. He's…he's just…he's very hot-tempered, Mr. Dillard, and he was devastated by what happened to Kasey. We all were, but Mike is a…he's a hard man."

"So you didn't tell him about our visit?"

"I was afraid. He's supposed to be in Greeneville at a cattle auction all afternoon."

She walked past me again as heavy steps echoed on the front steps. I stood and waited for the front door to open. When it did, the space was filled by a large, rugged-looking man with a long face and strong nose. His eyes were dark and liquid, almost smoldering. He was wearing a heavy denim coat, a gray cowboy hat, and work boots, and he wasn't smiling.

"Who're you?" he said as he stepped through the door.

"My name is Dillard," I said. "Joe Dillard." The look on his face told me not to offer my hand, and I didn't.

"Dillard. You're that lawyer."

"That's right."

"What are you doing in my house?"

"I was hoping we could talk."

"'Bout what?"

"Kasey."

He walked straight past me and disappeared into another room. Sandra lingered for a few seconds and then followed him. I could hear her muffled voice coming through the house, urgency in its tone. Then the heavy steps began again. He was coming back. The next thing I knew I was looking straight down the barrel of a shotgun. He had shouldered it and was aiming it at my forehead. It looked like a railroad tunnel.

"Easy, Mr. Cartwright," I said, holding up my hands. "Just go easy. All I want to do is talk."

"You ever come near my house again, you'll find yourself talkin' to the devil," he said. "Don't come around me or none of mine, including my wife. You understand me, mister?"

I started backing up. When I got to the door, I turned my back on him, waiting for the blast and the darkness that would follow. He'd left the interior door open, but the storm door was closed, and my hand was trembling as I reached down to turn the knob and push it open.

"Paul Milius is gonna burn in hell!" I heard him yell as I cleared the door and started down the steps. "And I hope you go with him!"

CHAPTER 19

While I was in northeast Tennessee looking down the barrel of a shotgun, Charlie Story was interviewing our client, Paul Milius. I asked her to secretly record and videotape the meeting for a couple reasons. First of all, I wanted to be able to see and hear the meeting and gauge Milius's reactions for myself rather than rely on Charlie's handwritten notes and recollections, and secondly, I wanted to cover our butts in case Milius made any baseless claims later on. As much as I hated it, I simply couldn't trust my own clients.

Milius walked in at the appointed time wearing a dark suit and tie. His driver remained in the lobby. Charlie was wearing a black and white, three-button jacket that looked almost like tweed and a black skirt. From the camera angle Charlie had chosen, I could see Milius's eyes light up when he saw her.

"My, my," Milius said as he took her hand, "Mr. Dillard didn't tell me you were so beautiful. Were you at the arraignment?"

"I was driving here from Johnson City," Charlie said.

"I would have noticed you."

"Please, have a seat," Charlie said. "Can I get you a bottle of water? It's all I have to offer."

"I'm fine," Milius said as he sat down. "I don't have a lot of time. Things are pretty crazy at work right now."

"I imagine they are," Charlie said.

"I'm spending most of my time trying to convince people that I'm not a murderer, and that I'm not going to spend the rest of my life in a prison cell. This has been terrible for business so far, and I'm afraid it's just getting started. God, you have beautiful eyes. I just had to say it."

"Thank you," Charlie said. "Now, if you don't mind, I'd like to get down to business."

"Ah, I see. All business. Okay, then, what would you like to talk about?"

"Women."

"One of my favorite subjects."

"I'm sure. I want to talk about Kasey Cartwright, and I want to talk about your wife, maybe some other things. I'm going to have to ask you some difficult questions, Mr. Milius, so I apologize in advance if I hurt your feelings or insult you."

Milius crossed his arms and raised his eyebrows. He leaned forward a bit in the chair.

"So you're going to interrogate me," he said.

"Something like that."

"You're going to ask about intimate details. My sex life."

"That could happen."

"Sounds delicious."

"How did you first meet Kasey Cartwright?"

"Kasey? Well, it's actually an interesting little story. I was in downtown Nashville at a fundraiser. It was one of those who's who events, everybody sucking up to one another. After I'd been there about an hour, this state senator from Jonesborough walks up to me and introduces himself. Name's Russell Poe, friendly enough guy. So after we talk for a minute, he says to me, 'Mr. Milius, I'm sure you probably get this kind of thing all the time and I'm actually a little embarrassed to ask, but would you mind taking a look at a short video I have on my phone?' I wanted to tell him to piss off, but I was polite and I told him I'd take a look.

"So he turns on the video and it's this beautiful young girl singing in a talent show at the Appalachian Fair in Washington County, and I can tell right away she's got *it*. A lot of people have talent, but very, very few of them have *it*. It's hard to explain, but she had a package, a combination of things that made her special. She was beautiful, she was genuine and humble, she had a subtle sexuality that made men yearn for her even though she was only fifteen at the time, her voice had a smooth, almost ethereal tone to it, and the instruments she played became a part of her. I recognized all of those things in that little two-minute clip he showed me on his phone. She was one in a million. So I asked him her name, got her contact information, and called her about a week later. I arranged to watch her do a set at a show in Newport, and then I made her an offer she couldn't refuse."

"Which was?" Charlie asked.

"A million dollars and the opportunity to work with and be developed by the best and fastest-growing record company in Nashville. We have the best songwriters, the best producers, the best sound engineers, the best studios, the best marketing people. You name it, we're the best at it. I talked to her and her grandparents about their concerns—things like her finishing high school where she was, things like her not touring too much until she graduated and whether she wanted to move on to college and whether we could work that in and make it happen. In the end, we decided to go slowly on the front end, but she decided she'd commit full-time to her music career as soon as she graduated from high school and worry about college down the road."

"I've been told that the million you say you gave her was a loan," Charlie said. "I've been told that musicians who get upfront money like that have to pay it back."

"It's advance money, standard operating procedure in the industry," Milius said. "They pay it back out of the royalties they earn. You have to understand that studio time and musicians and video productions and engineers and songwriters, all of those things are expensive."

"What if their record doesn't sell enough copies to pay back the million? Do they still have to pay it back?"

"It depends. Why are we talking about this? What does it have to do with Kasey's death?"

"Were there any financial disagreements between the two of you? Any disputes over royalties or earnings or contracts or anything else?"

"Zero. Nada. Kasey's music was selling. We were making money hand-over-fist. It was win-win for everybody."

"So there were no problems between you and her?"

"None."

"Then why did she toss a drink in your face back-stage at the CMT show?"

"So you heard about that…? She went off script during the broadcast, did a song she wasn't supposed to do. I confronted her about it. She said she wasn't going to sing party songs, wasn't going to sing about boys and trucks and drinking and bonfires. I told her that's the kind of thing that sells. She told me to get up there and sing it myself. I called her childish, and she tossed the tea in my face."

"What were you doing at her hotel room at two in the morning, after the after-party?"

"I just went up there to try and make up with her. To tell her I was sorry."

"Did you intend to have sex with her?"

"What? Are you kidding? She was eighteen. I'm married."

"So you had no interest in having a sexual relationship with her? You weren't having an affair with her?"

"You're starting to piss me off."

"If you weren't planning, or hoping, to stay, then why did you send your driver home? Why not just have him wait?"

"He'd been waiting all night. I didn't know exactly how long I'd be in her room, to tell you the truth. I just figured I'd call a cab. I *wasn't there for sex*, okay?"

"I don't believe you."

"Like I said, you're starting to piss me off."

"Get used to it. The prosecutor will be a lot worse than I am if you wind up taking the witness stand at trial."

"Kasey was too young," Milius said.

"You must not have thought the same thing about your wife when you started having sex with her. She was eighteen, wasn't she? Eleven years younger than you? Maybe you got tired of Lana and dreamed of the good old days. Thought you could relive the glory years."

"I *married* Lana, for God's sake. And I'm still married to her, in case you haven't noticed."

"How is it?" Charlie asked.

"How's what?"

"The marriage. How are you and Lana doing?"

"We're doing fine."

"Sex life good?"

"You are one coldhearted bitch, you know that? You should get into divorce law."

"You didn't answer the question," Charlie said. "How's your sex life?"

"Do you want times, places, length of encounter? Would you like to see my junk?"

"Yes to the times and places, no to the genitalia."

"Lana and I get together whenever we can, which is less often than I'd like," Milius said. "She's still hotter than a firecracker, but I'm busy. I work a lot of twelve-, fourteen-hour days, a lot of nights, a lot of weekends. And she drinks too much sometimes. But I still like to get in her pants every chance I get."

"Lana mentioned to Joe that there was some tension that night between you and her as well. What was going on?"

"She and I weren't getting along."

"Why not?"

"Same old same old. She was complaining about me spending so much time at work, and I was complaining about her spending so much time in a wine bottle. But when it comes down to it, I think Lana was probably feeling a little jealous, a little frustrated. Those big shows are hard on her ego. She used to be the diva, you know? She used to be the one up on stage getting all the attention and admiration. Now that she can't sing anymore, she just drinks. And she takes it all out on me."

"The nodes on the vocal chords?" Charlie said. "Must be tough for her."

"Yeah, it's been tough. She makes ten million a year sitting on her hands. I feel real sorry for her."

"Does she blame you?"

"Probably. She blames me for everything else that's bad in her life. Not that anything *should* be bad in her life. I mean, look how she lives. She has everything a woman could ever want."

"And you made all that possible."

"Damn right I did. Listen, I need to get going."

"But I'm not finished," Charlie said. "You haven't told me about the other women in your life, about your illegitimate children."

"That's none of your business," Milius said. "It has absolutely nothing to do with what happened to Kasey, has absolutely nothing to do with anything."

"But there have been other women, and there *are* illegitimate children," Charlie said. "That's relevant to us, Mr. Milius, because if we paint you as a loving and faithful husband who could not possibly have been in that room with adultery on his mind in front of the jury and then we put you on the witness stand, the prosecution is going to hand you your head on a platter. You understand that, don't you?"

"I understand that you're as mean a bitch as my wife."

"Don't be naïve, Mr. Milius. The press is all over this. Do you think for one second that they aren't going to find out about your affairs and broadcast them to the world? They will, you know. You're already a public figure, but the minute you were charged with murder, your life went straight under a microscope. If you have secrets, they'll soon be common knowledge. So how about dropping the act and being honest with me? It'll benefit you far more than it will hurt you."

Milius's shoulders slumped, and he seemed to melt a little, to get smaller. "What do you want to know?" he said.

"How many women have there been?" Charlie asked.

"Dozens. Too many to count. I'm sure I don't even remember all of them."

"How many children?"

"Four."

"Do you pay for them?"

"I have confidential agreements in place with all the mothers."

"Do you *pay* for them?"

Milius nodded his head slowly.

"How much?" Charlie asked.

"About $100,000 a month."

"And this is done through the court?"

"No," Milius said. "My lawyers handle it."

"So again, that night, did you intend to have sex with Kasey Cartwright?"

"I wouldn't say I intended to, but I wouldn't have run away if she'd been willing."

"You got up to her room sometime around two fifteen. Did you have a key?"

"No."

"So you knocked and Kasey let you in?"

"That's right."

"How long were you in the room?"

"Five minutes, maybe less."

"And during that five minutes or less, you slapped Kasey across the mouth."

Milius nodded again.

"Why? Why did you slap her?"

"Because she said something that made me angry."

"What was it?"

"None of your business."

"What did she say, Mr. Milius? It could be important."

Milius stood up and started walking toward the door. Just before he opened it, he turned back and faced Charlie.

"I'm not going to tell you or anybody else what she said. What I will tell you is this—what Kasey said to me had absolutely nothing to do with her death. She was alive when I walked out of that room."

CHAPTER 20

I t took me a couple days and a dozen phone calls to get what I thought was a good line on Ricky Church. He was eighteen years old and had been arrested twice for assault as a juvenile. He was still on probation for the last arrest, which involved him hitting a fellow band member between the shoulder blades with an electric guitar. He wasn't working, but he was attending a junior college during the day and playing music, alternating between the few goth bars in the Tri-Cities.

"His probation officer says he's playing at this place called The Shrunken Head in Kingsport," I said to Caroline as we sat at the dinner table. "I think I'll head over there and talk to him."

"The Shrunken Head?" she said, holding a fork with a piece of chicken dangling from a tine. "What kind of place is that?"

"Goth, I think."

"I don't want you going anywhere near a goth bar," she said. "Don't you remember what those goths did to that family out in the county a few years ago?"

She was referring to the first case I handled when I became an assistant district attorney. Three young goths, who also happened to be dabbling in Satan worship, had shot a family of four to death on a desolate county road, basically just for the hell of it.

"They aren't all like that," I said. "Most of them are artists, or wannabe artists. They just express themselves a little differently than the rest of us."

"When did you become such an expert?"

"I did a lot of research back then," I said, "and I looked into it a little more today. I haven't found anything that tells me this Ricky Church kid is a devil worshipper."

"Why don't you just go to his house? During the day? Like a normal person would?"

"Why are you being so surly? Are you hurting?"

Caroline took a lot of pain medication because the cancerous tumors had wrapped around her bones. She'd even had fractures in her spine and ribs by the time the metastasis was discovered. Her medicine cabinet looked like a junkie's wet dream, but she never seemed to be addled or confused or intoxicated. She did, however, get grouchy when the pain meds weren't quite doing the trick.

"I just don't want you going off to some freak show," she said.

"That's a little judgmental, don't you think? I've seen and known some pretty strange dancers over the years."

"What time would you have to go?" she said, ignoring my comment.

"Probably leave around midnight."

"Not a chance."

"They don't get going until midnight, Caroline. Midnight is *early* for them. And it's Friday."

"You're not going to go traipsing off to Kingsport to a goth bar at midnight," she said. "It's too dangerous."

"It isn't dangerous. It's just a bunch of kids listening to music and drinking and having a good time. And I wasn't planning to traipse. I thought I might drive."

She dropped her fork on her plate and looked at me like she wanted to choke me.

"You are...so...freaking...*frustrating* sometimes. You're half-crazy half the time, do you know that? You'll probably wind up in a fistfight. You've done that plenty of times, you know."

"And you're a fine human being, a perfect wife and mother, 120 percent of the time. Let's not argue, okay? I need to talk to this kid, and I want to do it in an environment where he feels and acts normal, even if it isn't normal to us. Let's just go on about our usual routine, you head on to bed around eleven, and when you wake up tomorrow morning, I'll be here safe and sound."

"Fine," she said, picking up her plate and carrying it to the sink, where she dropped it loudly. "But don't bother calling me when one of those ghouls starts eating your liver."

I had to give it to him—Ricky Church had that goth thing going on. I stood at the bar and drank a beer while he and his band played their first set. He was wearing combat boots and bondage pants with straps swinging everywhere, a black leather jacket with studs all over it and "Alien Sex Fiend" emblazoned across the back, a black T-shirt and black leather cuffs. His eyes were encircled by heavy, black eyeliner, and he had safety pins in both his eyebrows. His fingernails were all painted black, and he had shiny hoops in his ears. I had to give him something else, too—the boy could play the guitar. I wasn't a fan of the genre, which seemed to me to be a hybrid of punk and electric pop and heavy metal, but I knew the difference between a guitar player and a chord strummer. Ricky was all over those strings.

When the set was over, he unplugged from his amp, set his guitar on a stand, and stepped off the low stage. I walked up and stood in front of him. I wasn't dressed formally—just jeans and a pullover and a gray pea coat—but I felt as though I looked like the pope standing in the middle of a group of Hassidic Jews.

"Ricky Church?" I said to him.

"Yeah. Who are you?"

"Name's Dillard. I'd like to talk to you for a few minutes."

"About what?"

"Kasey Cartwright, mostly."

"Piss off."

"Piss off" is a phrase that has always pissed me off, and it did the trick again. I took a step toward Ricky, leaned in, and said, "I know Tom Kitchens real well. We're old friends." That was a lie. Tom Kitchens was Ricky's probation officer, and I didn't know him well at all. "Come over and talk to me now, or I'm going to call Tom first thing in the morning and tell him I saw you snorting cocaine in the bathroom."

"You can't—"

I grabbed his upper arm and pulled him toward me, and we walked out a side door into the chilly night. He fumbled for a cigarette and lit it while I looked him up and down. Beneath all that white foundation and black costume was a pretty good-looking kid. He was around five feet ten inches tall and had sharp, angular features. His eyes were light green.

"Are you a cop?" he said after he'd lit the cigarette.

"Lawyer."

"That's even worse."

"So they say."

"What do you want?"

"I want to know where you were on the night of December tenth."

"The night Kasey was killed?"

"Right."

"You think I killed her?"

"Where were you?"

"You're crazier than hell, man."

"Where were you? If I have to ask you again, you'll be on your knees, and you'll be in a lot of pain."

He looked me dead in the eye and said, "I didn't kill Kasey. I was in Nashville that night, but I swear I didn't kill her."

"What were you doing in Nashville?"

"She asked me to go to the show, the one where she performed," Ricky said. "It was a big deal to her. She got me tickets, and I invited a couple of my friends and went. It was awful, man. Sitting through two hours of that twangy crap made me want to throw up, but I did it for her."

"I thought you two had broken up."

"We had, but we were still friends."

"Have you talked to the police?"

"Haven't heard a word from them."

"Who went with you? I need names. When did you get to Nashville? Where did you stay? What did you do before and after the show? Run me through it."

He took a long drag off the cigarette and squinted at me through the smoke.

"Cody Taylor and Leslie Stewart went with me. Kasey and I used to double date with them once in a while. We checked into a Motel Six off I-40 around four o'clock, took a nap, and then went to a convenience store, and Cody bought a six-pack of beer. We drank it in the room and smoked a joint just before we left for the show. We got there just as it was starting, around seven thirty, and we hung out there until about nine thirty. Kasey had done her song, and I just couldn't take it anymore. We went downtown and hit a couple bars, hung out until around one in the morning, and then we went back to the room. We got up at eight the next morning and drove back home. Simple. End of story."

"Did you see Kasey or talk to her at the show?"

"She texted me a couple of times, but she was busy."

"What about after the show?"

"She texted me once and said she was going to some after-party, but she didn't invite me. She knew I wouldn't be comfortable around those country music types. That was the last time I heard from her. Who are you a lawyer for, anyway? Why are you asking all these questions? You planning on suing someone?"

"I'm representing the man accused of killing her."

He took another drag and choked on it. "Milius?" he said, coughing. "He's a piece of work, man. That's probably who killed her."

"Why? What makes you say that?"

"Because he was horny, man. He ran Kasey like a buck running a doe. All he wanted was to do her. He texted her all the time. She used to laugh about it, thought it was funny. But I'll bet you he killed her. He went up to her room and tried to do her, she told him to go jerk off in the corner, and he strangled her. That's what happened. No doubt in my mind."

"I'm going to check out every detail of your story," I said, "and if I find out you lied to me about anything, anything at all, I'll subpoena you to the trial and disembowel you in front of the jury."

He flicked the cigarette into the parking lot. "Do what you gotta do, lawyer man, but I didn't kill Kasey. She was one of my favorite people on the planet. Your client killed her."

I stood and watched him walk back into the club, disappointed that I'd learned even more about my client's sexual proclivities and that I hadn't developed an alternate suspect. I walked to my truck, started it, and was pulling out of the parking lot when I found myself humming the melody of one of the songs Ricky and his band had been playing earlier. The music really wasn't all that bad.

CHAPTER 21

'd never been one to develop stringent routines, but one of the few things I'd done on a regular basis over the years was jog along a trail that started near the back corner of my property and ran along a bluff above Boone Lake on a large piece of property adjacent to mine that was owned by the Tennessee Valley Authority. I always went in the mornings at sunrise or just a little while after, and on the Saturday morning after I talked to Ricky Church, I got up before daylight, drank a couple cups of coffee, read the newspaper (yes, I still read a document made out of paper that allegedly contained "news"), bundled up because it was thirty degrees outside, and called for Rio, my German shepherd, who came scrambling out of the bedroom through the house, his tail wagging like a helicopter blade. Rio loved going on the jogs, but he also loved the warmth and comfort of his pad in the bedroom, and he always waited until the last second before he rolled out of the sack.

I walked down to the trail while Rio ran around and peed on everything in sight, and I was grateful that the sun was peeking over the ridge to the east and that the wind wasn't blowing too hard. At forty-five, I was still in good shape, but in the winter when the wind got up and the temperature went down, the old joints sometimes let me know that I'd been hard on them for a long time. I started out at a brisk walk, and then after a quarter mile, broke into a jog. The leaves had fallen off the trees, but the forest on both sides of the trail was so thick it was still like running through a jungle. After I'd gone about a mile and was working up a pretty good sweat, I saw an unusual sight about fifty yards in front of me. A man was on one knee, apparently tying his shoe. Despite the fact that the land next to mine was owned by the TVA and was open to public use, I rarely saw anyone else on the trail. I slowed down to a walk and called Rio over. He always wore a harness, and I wrapped my right hand around it. Rio wasn't usually aggressive toward people unless they arrived at our house unannounced, but I didn't want to take a chance on him scaring or biting someone. As I got closer, the man switched knees and started tying and retying his other shoe. His back was to me.

"Coming up on your right," I said as I got close to him. "I have a big dog. Don't want to—"

At that second, the man made a quick move. I realized he was pointing something at my chest, but then my muscles stiffened and I was on my back, completely unable to move. I heard Rio squeal in pain beside me, but I couldn't turn my head to look in his direction. Then I was aware of men—several of them—rolling me onto my stomach. They were speaking in short bursts—Spanish, I believed. A knee pressed heavily on my neck as my arms, wrists, legs, and ankles were restrained. I heard Rio growl, and then I heard the sound of an engine coming to life, and then the world went black as someone pulled a bag of some type of light material over my head and secured it with a string around my neck. I was hoisted into the trunk of a vehicle and heard the lid slam shut. And then I was alone.

They tased me again as soon as they stopped the vehicle and opened the trunk. It had been less than thirty minutes since I was attacked on the trail. I was dragged out of the trunk and across what I thought was asphalt about fifty feet. I could hear another engine roaring before I was pulled up a short flight of stairs and into what I believed to be the passenger compartment of an airplane. They dumped me on the floor, where I lay struggling against the restraints and cursing under my breath until I heard the engine roar louder and felt the plane taxiing to the runway. Within minutes, I felt my stomach tighten as the plane—it had to be a jet—lifted off the ground and into the sky.

Once the plane was in the air, I was lifted to my feet, and two of the restraints were removed. I was still restrained at the wrists and ankles, but at least I was no longer trussed like a pig about to be barbecued. I was pushed a few feet and helped into a seat, and finally, the bag was removed from my head. I looked around me and saw eight men, all of them olive-skinned, dark-haired and dark-eyed, all of them wearing similar, paramilitary clothing. They were a stark contrast to the interior of the jet, which was almost as luxurious as the interior of Paul Milius's home.

"I'll kill every one of you sons of bitches if you hurt my dog," was the first thing that came out of my mouth.

"Your dog is unharmed, Mr. Dillard," said the man sitting closest to me. His English was accented, not heavily, but noticeably. His seat was facing mine, and he was leaning forward with his elbows on his knees. "We had to tase the dog and restrain him, yes, but we called your wife before we left the ground, and I'm sure she has attended to him by now."

"Who are you?" I asked.

"Names are unimportant," the man said. "We are taking you to someone who wants very badly to speak with you. If you cooperate, you'll be back home by tomorrow morning."

"Where are we going?"

"Somewhere far away. About thirty minutes before we land, which will be in about five hours, I'm going to have to ask you to allow us to replace the bag. It's for your own protection. In the meantime, I'll remove your restraints if you give me your word you won't attempt to do anything stupid. There are eight of us and only one of you. All the weapons have been stowed and locked away, and we'll be cruising at thirty thousand feet. There really is nothing you can do."

"What did you tell my wife?"

"The same as I told you. That you'll be back tomorrow, unharmed."

I looked around the cabin again. The men were all solid-looking, between the ages of thirty and forty. Every one of them was watching us and listening.

"All right," I said.

"All right what?"

"I give you my word I won't attempt to take over the airplane or jump out the window or kill anyone. How's that?"

Within seconds, I was free of the restraints.

"I suggest you try to relax and get some rest, Mr. Dillard," the man said. "When we get where we're going, you're going to be in the bed of a truck. We've tried to make it somewhat comfortable, but it's still going to be a long, rough ride."

CHAPTER 22

The mystery man was true to his word. Thirty minutes before the plane landed, he replaced the black bag over my head and the restraints on my wrists, although he allowed my hands to remain in front of me. When the plane rolled to a stop, I was ushered quickly out the door, down the steps, and across a tarmac where I was helped into the bed of a truck. There was a sheet of padded foam in the bed of the truck, and I was instructed to lie on my back and not sit up. I listened while some type of tarp was pulled tightly across the top of the bed. It smelled like canvas.

And then the ride began.

For the next ninety minutes, the truck went straight up. It was like being on a roller coaster that never went downhill. There were curves, dozens of them—hundreds of them—and switchbacks and huge potholes in the road that sent me bouncing like a pinball off the sides of the truck, the wheel wells, and the tailgate. I was grateful for the padding—they'd padded the bed of the truck like a cell in a mental institution—but I knew I'd be so sore I'd have trouble walking the next day. I'd taken the bag off my head early on, but the canvas over the truck bed had been pulled tight, and with the exception of a few small holes that let in tiny streaks of light, I was in complete darkness.

Finally, the truck came to a stop. I lay there quietly, waiting for what was to come next, when I heard the mystery man's voice.

"Mr. Dillard, have you removed the bag?"

"Yes."

"Please replace it. You cannot be allowed to see your surroundings. You'll understand soon."

Reluctantly, I pulled the bag back down over my face and secured the string.

"Are you ready?" he said.

"Ready."

"The bag is in place?"

"Yes, dammit! Let me out of here!"

A few minutes later, I was helped into yet another chair, and the bag was removed. I looked around and realized I was sitting in a garage, a residential garage that had room for four cars. There were the usual garage accoutrements around—tools, plastic bottles of oil, string-trimmer line—but there were no cars. All eight of the men who were on the plane were now in the garage with me. Directly in front of me was an empty folding chair. To my left was a door that led into a house, and within thirty seconds of the bag being removed, a young man walked through into the garage. He was average height and slim. His hair was short, jet black and wavy, his eyes liquid brown, his skin olive-colored like the rest of the men but not quite as dark. He sat down in the chair and looked me directly in the eye.

"Mr. Dillard," he said, "I apologize for all of this. My name is Alex Pappas, and the reason you're here is because I know Paul Milius didn't kill Kasey Cartwright."

"Will you take these off?" I said, holding up my hands.

"Certainly." Alex nodded, and the mystery man used a knife to cut through the plastic restraints.

"How do you know Paul didn't kill her?" I said.

"Because Lana forced me to set up a contract killing," he said. "She was supposed to pay $5 million, and the contractor was supposed to kill Kasey and Paul. Lana found out what hotel and what room Kasey was staying in, and she thought they would be in bed together. I don't know what happened in the room. All I know is that Paul was supposed to be dead on the night of the CMT show, and he's still alive."

"Tell me about the contract," I said. "How did it work?"

"It was real trade-craft stuff, straight out of a spy novel," Alex said. "Lana came to me first and told me if I didn't do what she wanted, she would make it appear as though I'd stolen $200,000 from Paul using an exclusive credit card he sometimes asked me to use on his behalf. She gave me a cell phone that she said had been encrypted and told me I'd be getting a text message in exactly two hours. When I got the text, it told me to drive immediately to the east side of the Percy Priest dam outside Nashville, take Stewart's Ferry Road to the parking lot, get out of my car, walk down toward the Stones River and wait.

"I did what the text said, and after I stood out there in the cold for about ten minutes, all of a sudden this guy appears out of nowhere. He's behind me, and he slides this package under my arm and tells me not to turn around. He says there's a laptop and a flash drive in the package and that I'm to upload the information I need to upload onto the laptop and send it to the email address that's provided. He said it was self-explanatory, and it turned out that it was. He also said that he was a professional and that the people he worked with were professionals and if I said a word to anyone about what was going on they would slit Tilly's throat and leave her lying on the steps of the state capitol. I'm not a violent man, Mr. Dillard. I'm no action hero. I almost wet my pants when he said that.

"So then he tells me that a bank account number and a bank routing number are also on the flash drive and that I'm to send the money to that account. I tell him I don't have any money to send, and he says, 'You will. Now go back to Franklin and do as Mrs. Milius tells you.'

"I drive back to Xanadu, and Lana stops me in the driveway and climbs into my car. She tells me to drive to Jim Warren Park in Franklin and park in an isolated spot. We find a spot, and she plugs a portable scanner into the USB port in my car. Then she hands me a typewritten sheet of paper, and on that paper is a lot of personal information about Paul Milius and Kasey Cartwright and the address of the Plaza Hotel along with a room number, a time, and a date. She tells me to open the laptop, plug in the flash drive, and start typing. I do what she asks. Then she tells me to hook the scanner to the laptop and scan in the photos she hands me. They're all of Paul and Kasey. I do it. She tells me to send the information and I send it. Then she gets out of the car, looks around for a few minutes until she's satisfied nobody is around, and she puts the photographs and the piece of paper on the ground and burns them.

"Once she's satisfied that everything is burned beyond recognition, she gets back in the car and tells me to drive across town to Liberty Park. It's mid-November and it's cold, so there's nobody there but us. Lana sits in the passenger seat, tells me to open the laptop again, and starts giving me a tutorial on opening a bank account in the Channel Islands. I don't know exactly how she did it, but it seemed to me that everything was pretty much preordained. A lot of it was already set up. The main thing she wanted from me was to get my name, address, and Social Security number on the account. It only took about thirty minutes, and the last thing she did was fund the account with a $5.1 million-dollar wire transfer. As soon as she gets confirmation that the money has hit the account, she tells me to do another transfer—two and a half million— to the routing number and account number that were on the flash drive I got from the guy at the river. I did it."

"So within a very short time," I said, "you went from innocent employee of Paul Milius to co-conspirator in a murder plot."

"And scapegoat if anything went wrong," Alex said. "Let's not leave out that important little detail."

"And now you're also a kidnapper," I said.

He nodded slowly. "Like I said, I'm sorry about that. I couldn't go back there. I was afraid to reach out to you any other way, and I'm lucky enough that my father has the resources to do something like this. I don't know who the contractors were or where they were located, but they had some high-tech toys, and I know they're probably looking for me. There's a little matter of some missing money that you probably don't know about."

"Enlighten me."

"I'm a pretty smart guy, Mr. Dillard, but at first I just didn't see a way out of this. I mean, Lana had set me up. I sent the information to the contractors, and I wire transferred the money that paid for the murder. I also knew exactly what I was doing, or at least I had a pretty good idea. I couldn't claim ignorance—the information was right there in front of me. If I told the police, I was going to jail. So I had to figure out a way to get out of there safely, to get Tilly out of there safely, and to maybe stick it to Lana a little in the process. It took me a few days, but I pulled it off."

"What did you do?"

"That laptop I told you about? Lana said I was to guard it with my life until after the job was done, and then she would instruct me on what to do with the rest of the money. After that, the rightful owners would reclaim the laptop. So I put it between my box spring and mattress. Then I discreetly reached out to my family and made some travel plans—on the same private jet that brought you here. It's owned by my father's company. Paul always gave me Thanksgiving off, and I usually went to New York to visit my parents, but Tilly and I told everyone we were going to just go spend a couple days at the Opryland Hotel, which didn't seem to raise any suspicion on Lana's part.

"We each packed a bag, got in my car, and drove to the airport, where we got on that beautiful jet and flew off to parts unknown. But before I left, I used what Lana had taught me, as well as some information I'd gathered since that day in the park, and set up an offshore bank account of my own. The last thing I did before I walked out of the house was pull the laptop out and transfer the rest of the money from the bank account Lana had made me set up to my new bank account. It's since been moved several more times. There was more than two and a half million dollars in that account, money that I assume was supposed to go to the contractors after Kasey and Paul were dead. I took every dime of it."

"I guess this means you're probably not going to voluntarily return and testify at Paul's trial."

"And admit to murder conspiracy, kidnapping, and to stealing more than $2 million? I don't think so."

"Are we in Ecuador?" I asked. "Rafael mentioned to me that one of your parents is from Ecuador. Your mother, maybe?"

"Yes, my mother," Alex said, "but you could be anywhere. My father is Greek and extremely wealthy, as is my mother and her family."

"These men speak Spanish," I said, glancing around the room. "It was uncomfortable as hell riding in the back of that truck, but it's pretty warm even though we're at a high elevation. The flight was about five hours in a jet that probably cruises around six hundred miles an hour. I don't think we're too far from the equator."

"If I don't tell you where we are, then you can truthfully deny knowing where I am if the need arises."

"Doesn't Paul know where you are? You worked for him for three years. Surely you told him about your family."

"Paul wasn't interested in my personal life," Alex said. "Paul was interested in business."

"So tell me again why you brought me here?" I asked.

"I wanted you to know the truth. Lana had Kasey killed and intended to kill Paul."

"But I can't *use* any of it. If you're not going to testify, everything you've told me is irrelevant. I can't go into court and tell the jury what you've told me."

"You can tell the district attorney and the police."

"Tell them what? That a man who, as you say, was part of a murder conspiracy, stole more than $2 million, and kidnapped me from my own backyard and flew me to God knows where, says Paul Milius didn't kill Kasey? Do you happen to know who did kill her?"

He shook his head, and his chin dropped to his chest. "I don't," he said. "There was no identifying information in the email I sent. The address was jibberish."

"Then without your testimony, this trip has been pretty much a waste."

"But at least you know Paul didn't do it."

"You were his personal assistant. Was he as promiscuous as I'm hearing he was?"

Alex nodded. "He was pretty much insatiable."

"What about Kasey? Did you hear or see anything that told you he was trying to seduce her?"

"I had my suspicions. He practically drooled on her every time he saw her."

"That's great," I said. "That's just great. I appreciate all the information. Can I go home now?"

The door opened again, and this time a woman walked through. She was beautiful, very much like Lana in terms of having a perfectly structured face and all the right curves in all the right places, although she was a bit taller than Lana and a bit thinner. She also had long, thick, brunette hair and eyes that were a deep, glossy brown. She was wearing tight, black jeans and knee boots and a white blouse.

"And you must be Tilly," I said. "Forgive me if I don't get up and shake your hand. I tend to lose my manners around people who kidnap me and haul me halfway around the world. I suppose you're also going to tell me what a terrible person Lana is but that, like Alex here, you're not going to come back to the good ol' U.S. of A. and testify."

"Lana and I grew up less than half a mile from each other, Mr. Dillard," she said. Alex got up from the chair he was sitting in, and she took his place. "We're first cousins. Her momma and my daddy are brother and sister. She's a year older than me, but we were inseparable. We went to the same schools, the same church. We rode horses together in shows for years on the weekends. I loved her like a sister. When she and Paul got married, nobody in the family approved because she was so young, and everybody boycotted the wedding. But I went. I was seventeen years old, and my daddy whipped my tail with a belt for doing it, but I went and I was her maid of honor. And then as soon as I graduated from high school, I went to work as her personal assistant. I toured all over the world with her and saw her career take off like a rocket. I was there when she got all the awards and sold all those records. I was there when the house was built.

"And then I saw Lana come crashing back down to Earth when she started having problems with her voice. I've seen the decline, Mr. Dillard, and to be perfectly honest with you, it breaks my heart because somewhere deep down inside of me I still love Lana. But you need to understand what you're dealing with. I think that's mainly why Alex went to all this trouble and expense to bring you down here—so we could try to get across to you that you're dealing with someone who is dangerous, someone who has become mentally ill and morally bankrupt, someone who has gone so far over the line now that she can't go back. She was responsible for killing Kasey, and she would have killed Paul if something hadn't gone wrong. And she's had help. That lawyer, that disgusting Carl Browning, has been helping her. I've heard them plotting. Be careful, Mr. Dillard. She'll kill you if she thinks she needs to. Don't doubt that for one minute."

"Why did she hire me?" I said. It was something I'd wondered about. If Lana had wanted Paul dead and it didn't work out, this murder charge seemed to be the perfect remedy for her. If he wound up being convicted, he'd be gone for a long, long time. So why hire me? Why not hire some rube who couldn't try a case?

"How did she find you?" Tilly said.

"Through a mutual friend, a sheriff. His name is Leon Bates. He's from the same county I'm from."

"I've met Sheriff Bates," Tilly said.

"Yeah, Lana mentioned that he'd stayed in the guesthouse."

"He and his girlfriend. What's her name, Erlene Barlowe? Redhead who owns a strip club? Calls everybody 'honey child' and 'baby doll'?"

"That's her."

"I don't mean to insult you, Mr. Dillard, but Lana thought Sheriff Bates and Miss Barlowe were charming hillbillies. I heard her talk about them more than once. It wasn't very flattering."

"She thinks they're stupid?" I said.

Tilly looked at the ground. "Like I said, I don't mean to insult you."

"So when Paul got arrested, she called Leon and he told her about me, which means she thinks I'm stupid, too?"

Tilly shrugged.

"Well I'll be damned," I said. "She hired me because she thought I was a rube. What will she do if I win? What will she do if I get him off?"

"She won't let you win, Mr. Dillard."

I stood and noticed a couple of the men around me stiffen.

"Is that right?" I said.

"I'm sure you're very good at what you do," Tilly said, "but I've seen Lana in action for a long, long time. You don't have a chance."

"We'll see about that," I said. "Alex, if you and Miss Hart have said everything you have to say, would you please have these men take me back where I belong? I've got work to do."

CHAPTER 23

The ride back from Ecuador (I was sure it had to be Ecuador) was uneventful. I had to wear the bag again when we rode down the mountain and got on the plane, but once we'd been airborne for a while, the mystery man allowed me to remove it, and I didn't have to wear it again. They even allowed me to sit up and ride in their rented car once we touched down at the Tri-Cities airport in Tennessee and got off the plane.

They dropped me in front of my house at around nine o'clock at night. I'd been gone since a little after seven that morning—roughly fourteen hours. When I walked in the door, I thought Caroline was going to break my neck hugging me. Sarah and Lilly and Randy and all the kids were there, too, and Rio almost knocked me down trying to slather me in dog spit. I regaled them all with the tale of my kidnapping, but I kept the most dangerous details about Lana Milius to myself.

I drank one beer and found myself dozing by ten o'clock. I barely heard the others leaving, and Caroline got me off the couch and helped me into bed, where I slept dreamlessly until I sat straight up at five the next morning. I was sore from bouncing around in the back of the truck the previous day, but I was able to get up and move around. I texted Leon Bates half an hour later: "Got anything for me?"

He texted back: "Behind the church. One hour."

Leon slid his long legs into the passenger side of my pickup right on time. We'd often met in the parking lot behind the old Highland Church of Christ. It was rural and isolated, and we'd never been bothered there.

"What's new, Brother Dillard?" Leon said as he removed his cowboy hat and laid it on the seat between us.

"Not much," I said. "I was kidnapped yesterday and flown to Ecuador, but other than that, things have pretty much been normal."

"I'm gonna assume you're pulling my leg," he said.

"No, no. It's true. I was running early yesterday morning, and the next thing I knew I'd been tased and hogtied and thrown in the trunk of a car. The car took me to the airport, where I was hustled onto a plane and flown three thousand miles away to visit a young man named Alex and a young woman named Tilly."

"Alex and Tilly? Aren't they Paul and Lana Milius's personal assistants?"

"They used to be. They have a new address now."

"Do you care to fill me in on the *who*s, *what*s, *when*s, *where*s, and *why*s of this little caper?"

"I don't know all the *what*s and *why*s," I said. "But I promise I'll tell you everything as soon as I figure it out. Tell me what you found out about my son-in-law."

"I put one of my best guys on him," Leon said. "He was off duty, of course, but you're going to need to compensate him for his time."

"Not a problem. What's the verdict?"

"Well, it's a bit complicated. The boy is apparently allowing himself to be led along by the nose a bit. This Tiffany Hill girl is a nurse at the medical center. Just graduated last year, twenty-five years old. Very, very attractive young lady. Lives by herself on the west side of town not far from where your daughter and son-in-law live. From what my man tells me, she is making no secret that she would very much like to have an affair with him. He also tells me that those sorts of things go on all the time in hospital settings. Nurses love to hate doctors, but they also love to catch one if they can."

"Even if the doctor is married and has a kid?"

"Some of them aren't too scrupulous about it."

"And I take it Randy isn't exactly fighting her off with a stick."

Leon folded his arms and rolled his head around a little.

"That seems to be a matter that's still up for debate," he said. "My man says he doesn't have any evidence that they're sleeping together or that they've slept together, but he also says he thinks it's just a matter of time. The girl has a bit of a reputation already, and she's working him hard. She calls him a lot. Shows up where he happens to be. If you're going to say something to him, my best advice is that now's the time."

"Thank you, Leon," I said. "I really appreciate this."

"So how far are you into this Nashville thing?"

"Far enough to know I'm up to my knees in BS," I said. "Oh, and by the way, I need to tell you something."

"What's that?"

"You know that guesthouse you and Erlene stay in when you go to the Miliuses' place? I interviewed all of Paul and Lana's employees, and one of them told me that Lana has video and audio recordings of everything that is said and done in there."

"Yeah," Leon said.

"Yeah? You're not worried about that?"

"Nah."

"Why not? Aren't you afraid some sex tape of you and Erlene will pop up in a political campaign somewhere down the road unless you pay somebody a bunch of money or do somebody a huge favor?"

"I ain't worried, Brother Dillard."

"Mind telling me why you're not worried?"

"Because Erlene's been doing that kind of thing for years. She spotted the cameras and the microphones less than five minutes after we got inside the house."

"So you got Lana to turn them off?"

"Not really. We kinda get a kick out of thinking Lana might be watching us sometimes."

"C'mon, Leon. Spill it."

"You're aware that Erlene has contacts all over this state and in lots of other states, too, correct?"

"I don't know the particulars, but yes, I imagine Erlene knows a lot of people."

"And I know a lot of people."

"Yes, I'm aware of that."

"And Lana Milius ain't no vestal virgin, am I right?"

"I couldn't comment on that."

"I can. She ain't. And Erlene has proof. So we already have an unwritten agreement. Erlene took care of it right away."

"Enough said, Leon. Don't tell me anything else."

"You shouldn't have brought it up."

"I was just trying to help."

"That you were. So back to Paul Milius. You gonna be able to get him off?"

"I have absolutely no idea. I'll let you know as soon as I find out."

"And when do you expect that will be?"

"When the jury comes in with a verdict."

CHAPTER 24

I was waiting just inside the hospital cafeteria door when Randy came walking in. He was wearing his white coat, accompanied by a young man and two young women, also wearing white coats. He turned and said something under his breath when he saw me, and they walked on.

"I need a minute of your time," I said to him.

"I don't have much."

"Won't take long. Can we step outside?"

There was a small courtyard outside the cafeteria with five small tables and about a dozen chairs. It was empty because the temperature was below forty degrees, and the day was blustery and dim. After we'd walked about twenty feet from the door, I turned and planted myself in front of him, less than a foot away.

"I know what you've been doing," I said.

"What? What are you—?"

"Tiffany Hill ring a bell?"

His jaw went slack, and the color left his face. "I don't know what you're—"

"Yes, you do. Nurse. Pretty nurse. Word is she's looking for a doctor. That kind of thing happens a lot from what I've been told. She was in your car the night you wrecked, and the two of you have been spending some sneak-around time together. How am I doing?"

"Have you been *following* me?"

"I don't have time to follow you. I paid somebody to do it."

"You paid somebody? That should be illegal or something. I'm not…I'm not having this conversation."

He turned to walk away, but I grabbed the sleeve of his coat and spun him back around.

"You're going to stand here and listen to what I have to say, or I'm going to kick your ass all over this courtyard," I said.

"You wouldn't dare," he said. "There are witnesses all over the place."

"Yeah, and those witnesses are going to tell the cops that the old guy beat the living shit out of the young guy while the young guy is being carted off in an ambulance."

I meant every word of it, and he could obviously tell I meant it because he didn't offer to move. He stood there looking at the ground.

"You don't love my daughter anymore? That's fine, Randy. It happens. People fall in love. People fall out of love. You don't want to stay with your son and be part of a family anymore? That's fine, too. My old man abandoned his family. Scumbags do it all the time. But if you don't love my daughter and if you don't want to be a part of a family anymore, you're going to do it the right way. You're going to go to Lilly, you're going to look her in the eye, and you're going to say, 'Lilly, I don't love you anymore. I want a divorce.'

"Then you'll get a lawyer and Lilly will get a lawyer and they'll act like they're being nasty and battling for you, but all they'll really be doing is running up the tab and having a drink together after work. In the end, they'll make a standard financial deal and a standard child custody deal and you'll be able to tell your new girlfriend what a bitch your ex-wife and her lawyer were and how badly you got screwed in the settlement.

"Then in a few years, your wife, who didn't care to break up your family, will start looking around to break up another family. Maybe you won't make enough money to suit her. Maybe your house won't be big enough or your cars won't be nice enough or your pecker won't be big enough to suit her. She knows you're married, right? She knows you have a child, right? What's she telling you? What's her pickup line? That she thinks you might be soul mates?

"Here's the thing, and I want you to listen closely to me right now. You're a young guy, you're good-looking, and you'll soon be a doctor, which means you're going to be relatively wealthy unless you turn out to be a lousy money manager. You're going to have women make plays for you. Some of them will be subtle, some of them will be overt, but all of them will be empty. And what you have with Lilly is not empty. I've seen you two together for what, seven years now? Lilly loves you the same way Caroline and I love each other. There is nothing she wouldn't do for you. She cherishes you and everything that goes with you. You're a wonderful father. Joseph's eyes light up every time he sees you.

"I'm afraid you're about to make a terrible, terrible mistake. You've been under a huge amount of pressure with school for the past three years. The baby wasn't planned. The marriage was because of the baby. You got into a car accident a few months back and wound up inadvertently addicted to opiates, and God knows an opiate addiction is a tough thing to overcome. I thought you'd kicked it, but it's obvious you haven't. We'll get you more help. And now you have this pretty girl going, 'Hey, hey, look at me and how pretty I am. I can put some spice into that mundane, pressure-cooker life of yours and make you feel better at the same time.' But like I said, she knows you're married. She knows you have a baby. What kind of person does something like that? Answer me, Randy. What kind of person breaks up a new marriage with a young child?"

"I…I don't know what to say. I think I'm just—"

"From what my hired spy tells me, you haven't slept with her yet. Is that true?"

"What? Have I what?"

"Have you slept with her?"

"No. She wants to, but—"

"Then it isn't too late. If you'd slept with her, I'd tell you to go to hell. You can fix this if you want to. You go to Lilly, you tell her what you've done, you tell her the girl was in your car the night you wrecked, and you tell her you're sorry. But you only do it if you mean it. Lilly will forgive you, eventually. She'll be angry at first, she might even kick you out of the house for a little while, but she'll forgive you and then you can go on from there. Are you listening to me, Randy? Look at me."

He looked up at me. A tear had slipped from his right eye and was running down his cheek. I felt sorry for him.

"You have to deal with the opiates, and you have to stop drinking," I said. "If you don't, you won't have a chance."

He nodded slowly. "I know," he said. "I'm trying."

"Don't try. Do it. I have to go back to Nashville tomorrow. When I get home, we're going to have another conversation, and you're going to tell me that you came clean with Lilly and that you're clean on the pills and the booze. I'll probably already know if you talk to Lilly because the first thing she's going to do is tell Caroline, but you and I are going to get together again when I get back."

"Fine."

"We'll work through this together, Randy. That's what families do. They face problems together and they overcome them."

CHAPTER 25

Walking into the main hospital entrance at Vanderbilt University always gave me the jitters. I'd been there dozens of times, and I realized all the people who worked there were well-meaning and kindhearted, but I hated the place. It made my stomach churn. It made my head ache. It made my vision narrow.

Caroline had ridden down with me on Milius's jet late on the previous afternoon. I thought we'd make a joint trip of it. I had some work to do, and she had a bone scan scheduled.

When we landed at Xanadu, I introduced Caroline to Lana and told Lana we'd rented a room at the Opryland Hotel. All we needed was for somebody to drive us to the airport so that I could rent a car. She wouldn't hear of it. When I politely but firmly declined her offer of a driver to carry us around town, she gave me the keys to a black BMW 7 series sedan. We drove to the motel and checked in, had a wonderful dinner at a place on Demonbreun Street called Etch, and then went down to Broadway and bar-hopped through a few of the honky-tonks drinking cold beer and listening to live country music. One of the places, Tootsie's, had three floors with a separate bar, a separate stage, and a separate band on each floor. It was a blast except for when the musicians would come around the audience and beg for money. They were aggressive about it. It was annoying because it made me feel like I was being hustled.

Caroline's bone scan was scheduled for ten o'clock the following morning. At eight, we walked into the radiology department, and she was injected with a radioactive dye. We went out and got some breakfast and were back two hours later. During those two hours, the dye was supposed to attach itself to cancerous cells in Caroline's body, and then later, when they ran her through the scanner, the cancer cells would light up like flashlights on the computer monitor above the scanner.

I'd sat through eight bone scans over the prior two years. Caroline would be helped onto a table that slid her through the scanner, and I'd sit in a chair a few feet from her and watch the monitor. The results hadn't changed—meaning the tumors hadn't grown—in nearly two years because the combination of drugs and hormones they were treating her with were working. The scans normally took about twenty-five minutes. Less than five minutes into this one, I knew something had changed, and I knew it wasn't for the better.

The scanner started at her head and slowly produced an image of Caroline's skeletal system. I knew there was a tumor on her skull and one in her right shoulder—I'd seen them every single time I'd watched a scan. But this time, the tumor in her skull seemed to be larger. It seemed to be brighter than normal. So did the tumor in her shoulder. I sat there and kept my mouth shut, though, because I wasn't certain. When the scanner began to move down her body, my hands started to shake. Just below her right elbow was a bright glow that I hadn't seen before. The tumors in her spine seemed to be unchanged, but her pelvis, which had been clear of tumors in the past, was now covered in luminescence. I nearly choked when I heard her say from the table, "How does it look, baby?"

"Looks good," I lied. "Don't see any change."

There were more. On both of her femurs, on both tibias and fibulas, even in her feet. I got up and took a couple steps toward the monitor and peered at it, not wanting to believe what I was seeing.

"All good?" Caroline said.

"Yeah. Yeah, it looks the same as always."

"You're lying to me, Joe. I can hear it in your voice."

"I'm not a radiologist. There are a couple things that might be a little different. Let's just wait and hear what the doctor has to say."

A little over two hours later, after the scan had been read and the results interpreted and passed along to Caroline's oncologist, we received the kick in the gut.

"It's on the move again," Dr. Abrams, Caroline's oncologist, said, "but don't panic. It isn't out of control."

"You just said it's on the move," I said while Caroline cried softly beside me. "Doesn't sound to me like it's *under* control."

She patiently explained that cancer cells sometimes morph and become resistant to treatment over time, and that was what seemed to be happening. The cancer was still confined to her bones, however. It hadn't spread to her brain or her heart or her lungs. And there were other treatment options available.

"I want to put her in a clinical trial with a drug called exemestane and another called enzalutamide," the doctor said. "It's my study, it's here at Vanderbilt, and she's perfect for it."

* * *

Several hours later, Jack and I were driving down Briley Parkway in his car. We'd had dinner at the hotel with Caroline and Charlie, we'd talked the latest cancer development through, and Jack and I had gone out, ostensibly to get some dip, which was a habit Jack picked up during his college baseball days and had yet to quit. The mood was dark; both of us were angry and frustrated and terrified about what might happen to Caroline. We were tired of the roller coaster ride that goes along with loving someone who has cancer. We'd talked about it a little, but mostly we were just driving around in silence, watching the reflections from headlights bounce and slide through the night. Jack had downed four beers during dinner, and I could smell it.

"I should be driving," I said.

"I'm all right."

"I'm stone sober."

"I'm all right, Dad. Don't worry about it."

"So how's it going between you and Charlie?" I asked. "You two getting serious?"

"I spend an awful lot of time thinking about her," Jack said. "She reminds me a lot of Mom. She's just so *good*, you know?"

"Have you guys talked about the future?"

"A little, but right now I just want to finish up with law school, pass the bar, and then we'll figure it out. I can tell you this, though. The future I imagine always has her in it."

Just then, a tricked-out, silver coupe with a loud muffler raced up on our right, passed us, and cut back in front of us, nearly striking Jack's right-front fender.

Jack swore aloud while I watched the car careen back and forth through the lanes ahead of us, cutting off other cars, causing people to slam on their brakes and blow their horns.

"Son of a bitch," Jack said, and I felt myself being pulled back into the seat as he gunned the engine.

"What are you doing?" I said.

"Wrong place, wrong time," Jack said. "For him."

"Don't. Just let it go."

But within seconds, Jack had closed the distance and was five feet from the coupe's rear bumper. He turned his lights on bright and started blasting the horn.

"Jack! Knock it off!" I reached over and put my hand on his shoulder, but he wouldn't look at me. I could see the anger in his face.

We'd followed the coupe for about fifteen seconds when it suddenly veered off to the right and shot down a side street. Jack was still right on the car's tail. Although I couldn't be certain, it looked like there was one person in the car, a male wearing a baseball cap.

"I hope he pulls over," Jack said. "I'm gonna stomp him flat."

"Calm down," I said, but I, too, had started to feel an adrenaline rush. Like Jack, I was looking for an excuse to unleash some pent-up anger, and this unsuspecting thug seemed to be just the ticket.

Suddenly, the coupe did a ninety-degree turn into a parking lot and stopped. I looked around. It was a church. Zion Baptist. I saw the driver's door open. Jack clicked out of his seat belt and was out of the car. I did the same.

The guy who came out of the car was wearing jeans and a black jacket. A Cincinnati Reds baseball cap with a straight bill sat at an angle on his head. He was maybe five feet ten and stocky, around a hundred and eighty pounds. He had a narrow, closely trimmed beard. In his right hand was a tire iron.

"I'm gonna take that thing away from you and shove it up your ass," I heard Jack growl. Before I could get around the car, before I could do or say anything, Jack was on the guy. Jack was about an inch shorter than me at six feet two, but he was a lot thicker. I'd seen him bench press three hundred and fifty pounds like it was a toothpick. I'd seen him squat six hundred pounds and deadlift more. He was quick, too, and at that moment, he was eaten up by anger. He was frightening, even to me. He charged the guy like a bull and had him off his feet before he could swing the tire iron. Jack's right arm wrapped under the guy's hips while his left hand controlled the arm that held the tire iron. Jack lifted him in a fireman's carry, took two steps, and slammed the guy across the back windshield of the coupe like a wet towel. I heard the guy let out an "Ugh," and the tire iron clattered off the roof of the car and onto the asphalt. Jack stepped back about a foot, grabbed a handful of jacket with his left hand, pulled, and punched the guy in the mouth with his right fist so hard that I heard his teeth crack. He was reloading his fist to hit the guy again when I jumped between them and locked up Jack's shoulder.

"Enough!" I said. "Enough! You're going to kill him."

He was so amped up that he tried to throw me aside, but I clung to him like a bull rider.

"Easy," I said. "Easy, easy. Get a hold of yourself."

He looked at me, recognized me, and I knew he was back. He was breathing heavily, and his eyes looked as big as silver dollars.

"Get in the car," I said. "Passenger side. We need to get out of here."

I took him by the arm and walked him around the car. The passenger door was still open, and I stood there while he slid inside. Then I walked over to the thug. He was still lying on his back, his eyes open in a blank stare. His mouth was bleeding heavily and I noticed a couple bubbles as he breathed. I grabbed the front of his coat and pulled him off the trunk of the car.

"Can you walk?" I said as he moaned in pain. "Yeah, that looked like it probably hurt. My guess is you've got a broken rib or two. Probably have to get some work done on your grill, too." As I was dragging him to the front seat, I spotted the tire iron lying on the asphalt a few feet away. I dropped him onto the driver's seat of his coupe then walked over, picked up the tire iron, carried it to where he was sitting, and set it in his lap.

"Might want to watch how you drive in the future," I said as I closed his door. "You never know when somebody's mother might be sick."

CHAPTER 26

Jack had been making the rounds in the country music industry, and after he went ballistic on the thug in the parking lot, I asked Jack to tell me about his latest interview. He'd mentioned it earlier but we hadn't had a chance to talk, so I rolled the car onto Briley Parkway and cruised while he talked and wound down.

The industry was a tough nut to crack because people in the business were cliquish and paranoid and self-important. Jack, however, was able to say he was working for Paul Milius's lawyer, and because he had developed some pretty good telephone skills, he wasn't afraid to be assertive when the need arose. He'd also had the good sense to go out and get some official-looking identification made, so he was granted a few audiences. The only one of any real value was with an up-and-comer named Derek Birch, a long-legged, dope-smoking, Jack Daniels drinker who considered himself a rebel, an artist, and the most important country music icon of the young century. Kasey Cartwright had toured with him for two months during the summer when she was sixteen, but Birch had since switched from Paul Milius's label to another record company. Jack had been told that Birch didn't much care what anyone thought about him and would give an honest—if not drug-and-alcohol-addled—opinion on most anything. Jack didn't audio or videotape his conversation with Derek Birch, but he took detailed notes, and I was satisfied that he recounted it for me accurately.

Jack walked into Birch's backstage dressing room at around nine thirty on a Friday night at the Bridgestone Arena in downtown Nashville. Birch was the headliner, wrapping up a six-month tour, and was scheduled to go on stage at ten thirty. There was a large makeup mirror in the antique-white room, a couple stools, a leather couch against the far wall, and two acoustic guitars on stands. Birch was sitting near the mirror with a red Solo cup in his hand, wearing a denim shirt, denim jeans, and cowboy boots. He had dark, aviator sunglasses on and a John Deere cap pulled tightly down over his head. He had a male model chin, with a jawline and teeth to match. The air in the room was thick with marijuana smoke. Jack noticed a tall, decorative glass bong sitting on the counter near the mirror. Next to it was a handle of Jack Daniels, a two-liter bottle of Coke, and a small cooler filled with ice.

"Yo, what's up?" Birch said as Jack walked cautiously into the room. "Close that door behind you and lock it so we can have some privacy."

A band called Buick Five was on the stage, and the rockabilly was blasting. Closing the door didn't muffle the sound completely, but it made it possible for Jack and Birch to talk without having to shout. Jack, who had dressed in country music concert gear—jeans, flannel shirt, boots, cowboy hat—shook hands with Birch, who motioned for him to take a seat on the couch. As soon as

Jack was seated, Birch picked the bong up, walked over, and offered it.

"No, thanks," Jack said.

"Don't smoke?"

"I'm working tonight."

"So am I," Birch said. "You ain't one of them tight asses, are you?"

"No, no," Jack said, but then he smiled. "Well, maybe. I'm wound pretty tight most of the time."

Birch laughed. "At least you're honest," he said. "Sure you don't want to hit this? It'll mellow you right out."

"Not right now," Jack said. "Maybe later."

"So my agent tells me you're working for the lawyer who's defending Paul Milius," Birch said. "Says the lawyer is actually your dad."

"That's right," Jack said. "I'm in my last year of law school."

"You're a big dude, so please don't get up and kick my ass for what I'm about to say, but I've never met a lawyer who had a soul, man. Do they surgically remove it in law school, or do you lose it later on?"

Jack shrugged his shoulders. "I know what you're saying," he said. "But I think my dad's okay. He's been at it for a long time, and I think he's been able to keep his soul. Most of it, anyway. And I don't think I've lost mine. At least not yet."

"Then you're as rare as a well-lived life, man. Hope you can keep it that way. I was just thinking about our culture and how bankrupt it's become before you walked in. Gave me an idea for a new song. I'm going to call it 'Empty Malls.'"

"Empty Malls?" Jack said. "What's it going to be about?"

"I'm just going to write a tune about an empty mall in the South, and how it's this big, empty shell covering the scattered shards of our broken retail dreams."

"Sounds depressing," Jack said.

"It *is* depressing, man. We're depressing. But it's the freakin' truth."

"Speaking of truth," Jack said. "There are some things I'd like to talk to you about."

Birch popped off the stool and started pacing in a circle.

"Now that was lame, dude," he said. "Bad, bad segue. We're sitting here rapping, establishing some trust, talking about empty malls and bankrupt dreams, and you go and try to slide that awful segue in there. I should just go ahead and have the security guys come toss you right now."

"I'm sorry," Jack said. "I'm just not used to…I haven't talked to anyone like you in a while. Hell, I've never talked to anyone like you in my life. By the way, there are cops all over this place. Don't they mind that you're smoking dope in here?"

"They're not on duty, man. They're freelancing. We pay them. We can do whatever the hell we want as long as we don't kill anybody."

"Speaking of killing somebody…." Jack smiled again, and Birch slapped his knee and went back to his chair.

"Okay, lawyer's son," Birch said as he picked up the bong, lit it, and took a long pull. "You seem to be honest, and you've got a sense of humor. What do you want to talk about?"

"I'd just like you to tell me what you know about Kasey Cartwright and Paul Milius."

Birch blew the smoke out slowly and set the bong back down. He picked the Solo cup up and took a long drink. Jack could smell the whiskey from five feet away.

"Kasey came out on tour last year for a while before I left Paul's label," he said.

"Why'd you leave?" Jack asked.

"Just a creative-differences thing, man. Happens all the time. But Kasey, she'd open the night, do about an hour, then she'd come to my bus or to my dressing room and get high with me when the show was over. Earthy chick, you know? All about what was natural, at least that's what she wanted people to think. But she liked the retail dreams. She wanted to make as much money as she could. Wanted the fancy houses and cars and all that. She used to talk to me about it all the time. 'What's fair? How much can I make doing this or that? Is Paul screwing me?'"

"Was he?" Jack asked.

"Screwing her? Financially, a little I'm sure. The new ones always get screwed. Physically, definitely."

"So he was having sex with her?"

"Absolutely, man."

"How do you know for sure?"

"Because I saw them getting it on in her trailer. I have this little habit of wandering around after shows. Harmless creepin', you know? Helps me wind down. Sometimes I like to look in windows, check out what people are doing. I saw them doing the nasty, man, with my very own eyes. But Kasey had already told me she was doing him, which is the main reason I wandered over that way that night. I just couldn't resist the chance of getting to see Kasey naked. Did you ever see her? I mean when she was alive?"

"All I've seen is pictures," Jack said. "Pretty girl."

"Sensuous, too," Birch said. "But anyway, Kasey thought she was playing Paul so she could make more money. I didn't have the heart to tell her she was just an amusement to him, just a temporary thing. But ol' Kasey, she got tired of Paul before Paul got tired of her. She started seeing Cameron Jones as soon as she turned eighteen."

"Cameron Jones is another singer on Paul's label, right?"

"Yeah, good buddy of mine, Cameron. Good artist, too. A little more old-school than me, not as edgy, but still good at what he does."

"Did Paul know Kasey was seeing Cameron?"

"Yeah, yeah. Cameron said Kasey was upfront about it. It was kind of funny. What he told me was that she went all John Hancock about it. I'd never heard that phrase before."

"Did Cameron say how Paul reacted?"

"Paul doesn't like to lose. He didn't get where he's at by letting people take what he thinks is his. Cameron said Paul wasn't none too happy about it."

"Unhappy enough to kill Kasey?"

"I guess that's the million-dollar question, isn't it? I'm sorry, but I don't have any answers for you. Listen, man, it's getting close to show time, so if there isn't anything else, I need to start getting my voice warmed up and let my makeup girl put my stage face on."

Jack rose from the couch and reached out a hand to Birch.

"Thanks," Jack said. He didn't say anything about sending Birch a subpoena. It might not happen, but Birch said he had actually seen Paul Milius and Kasey having sex. That was admissible in court. Jack just didn't know whether there would be any use for the testimony. And since Cameron Jones had apparently stepped in and lured Kasey away from Paul, Cameron might be a candidate for the SODDI defense. Maybe it had been worth the time and trouble to talk to Derek Birch.

"Sure you don't want to hit this bong before you head out?" Birch said.

"It smells really good," Jack lied, "but I think I'll pass."

* * *

"That was a pretty good story," I said as I made a U-turn at a red light and started back toward the hotel, "but make sure you don't tell it to anyone else. Have you told Charlie?"

"Not yet," Jack said. "We've both been pretty busy."

"Don't tell her."

"Why not?"

"Because I don't want Birch anywhere near the court-room. I don't want the police or the prosecution to get even a whiff of that story. As far as I know, they suspect that Paul and Kasey were having an affair, but they can't prove it. Let's keep it that way."

CHAPTER 27

Caroline and I spent the next morning at Vanderbilt going from office to office, getting blood work done, going through the process of enrolling Caroline in the clinical trial. She was red-eyed and lethargic, largely because she'd spent much of the previous evening crying in our hotel room. She was scared, but more than that, she was upset because she felt as though she'd let everyone in the family down by allowing the cancer to advance, as though she had any choice at all in the matter.

Late in the morning, I took Caroline back to the Opryland Hotel so that she could take a nap, and I drove to the district attorney's office near the courthouse downtown. Their offices were on the fifth floor, and after going through security, I was directed by a middle-aged woman to a large but practical office overlooking the Cumberland River. In the office waiting for me were Ronnie Johnson, the district attorney general of Nashville, Pennington Frye, the assistant handling the Paul Milius case, and a detective named William Smiley. All three men were dressed in dark business suits, as was I. I'd had only a brief encounter with Frye at Milius's arraignment and had never met Johnson or Smiley. We all shook hands and exchanged small talk for a few minutes while we tried to get some kind of read on one another.

"So how about this case?" Johnson said as the small talk wound down. He seemed friendly enough with his mouse colored-hair and salesman attitude. "What are the chances of getting some kind of plea worked out?"

"What's on the table?" I asked. "Involuntary manslaughter? Negligent homicide? We might be able to talk about something like that."

"So you're saying he killed her by accident?" Johnson said.

"I'm not saying anything at all. I'm just asking about possibilities."

"I don't think we're ready to offer anything yet," he said.

"I'm not really looking for anything yet," I said. "Of course, that might change if you guys drop some kind of bomb on me."

Everyone laughed nervously. Prosecutors were required by the law to disclose everything to defense attorneys in criminal cases, but everyone knew they didn't do it.

"Have you come across anything exculpatory?" I asked. Exculpatory evidence tended to point toward a defendant's innocence.

"Not a thing that I'm aware of," Johnson said. He looked at the other two men. "Penn? Bill? Anything exculpatory?"

Both men shook their heads at the same time. "I would have provided anything exculpatory," Pennington Frye said. "I'm not one of those win-at-all-cost guys."

That statement told me that Pennington Frye was exactly what I feared he'd be—a win-at-all-costs guy. Otherwise, he would have simply said, "No," in response to Johnson's question. I couldn't really blame him, though. This was a huge case for Frye, and a huge case for their office. It involved a country music star and a celebrity record company owner, it was in the state capitol, and the media scrutiny had been intense. I was able to avoid the media for the most part because I wasn't from Nashville, and I could tell them to stuff themselves if they got too close. I didn't need them. But for a public employee, a prosecutor, well…careers were made and broken on this kind of case. The only thing that would have made it even more volatile would have been if an election had been pending. Thankfully, Ronnie Johnson was only two years into an eight-year term. No election pressure on this one. Just reputation pressure, and in Nashville, reputation was important.

"It's pretty thin for a murder case," I said. "All you really have is the DNA match."

"Those DNA matches are pesky things for defendants," Johnson said from behind his wide-topped, oak desk. "And you're right. Without it, we wouldn't have much at all. But we have it."

"All it proves is that he slapped her," I said.

"I beg to differ," Johnson said. "It also proves he was there at or near the time of the murder, which was very late at night. He was the last person to see her alive. It proves he was agitated enough to strike a young woman in the face, a woman he'd been pursuing romantically for quite some time. How big a step is it, really, to grabbing her by the neck and choking her?"

"You're planning to get into all the sexual stuff at trial?" I asked.

"As much as the court will allow. I think it gives the case some texture, allows the jury to put things into perspective."

"I'll fight you every step of the way on it," I said. "Unless you have something that proves he'd been 'pursuing her romantically,' as you said. Oh, and he says he didn't do it, for what it's worth. He's very convincing."

Johnson chuckled. "Let him tell it to the jury. We'll see how they feel."

"I understand you have a couple items in your possession that might be of interest to me," I said.

Johnson looked at Frye and Smiley again and held up his hand as if to say, "I got this." He leaned forward, put his arms and elbows on his desk, and folded his fingers.

"Let me guess," he said. "You're talking about a cell phone and a diary, both property of Kasey Cartwright."

"Exactly. Can I take a look?"

Johnson shook his head. "Sorry. There's nothing there for you."

"How about letting me judge that for myself?"

"We're not planning to use the diary or the phone or anything either one of them contains at trial," Johnson said. "And because of that, I don't have to let you examine them if I don't want to. The rules don't require it, and I'm not going to do it."

"But you have them in your possession?" I asked.

Johnson nodded.

"Then I'll file a motion and ask the judge to order you to let me examine them."

"File away, Mr. Dillard. We both know the judge will tell you you're not entitled to them. But I will tell you this—the information contained in the diary and the cell phone is more damning than exculpatory. Your client is a vulgar womanizer. But the diary is hearsay, and it would be impossible to authenticate the cell phone messages since your client used a prepaid, disposable cell when he communicated with the victim. The cell her grandmother gave us is also a pre-paid. I assume your client gave it to her. But again, we're not going to use them. Do you have anything specific for Detective Smiley or Mr. Frye?"

"I don't believe I do," I said, thinking the meeting was about to be cut off.

"Then I'm going to ask them to excuse themselves so you and I can talk privately," Johnson said.

A couple minutes later, Frye and Smiley were gone, and the door had been closed tightly. Johnson walked around the desk and took a seat in the chair Frye had just vacated, just a few feet away from me.

"Has Paul told you we're friends?" he said.

"He mentioned it in passing, but we really haven't gotten a chance to talk about it," I said. "And I heard you call him a vulgar womanizer just a second ago if I'm not mistaken."

"He *is* a vulgar womanizer, but he's still my friend. I hate this for him. He was extremely generous to me when I was running for this office, and he's been extremely generous to a lot of my political friends. But I hope you'll understand, and I hope you'll pass this along to him, that I had no choice. It was such a big stage, there was so much media interest, that I had to do it by the book. I turned everything over to Penn, and Penn and Bill Smiley presented the case to the grand jury. And I can understand why the grand jurors returned an indictment. Paul and this girl were having an affair, or at least one that had recently ended, they got into a public scrap at the CMT Awards show, the bad feelings continued and spilled over into the after-party, he went to her hotel at two in the morning and sent his driver home, and then a maid found her dead with a chunk of his skin wedged between her teeth. You were a prosecutor once, from what I understand, Mr. Dillard. What would you have done?"

I thought about saying, "I would have checked out his wife very carefully," but I kept it to myself. I'd never been one to show any cards to the prosecution before a trial.

"It sounds like you did what you thought was right," I said. "I'll pass that along."

"Thank you," Johnson said, "and pass along the information about the diary and the cell phone. A lot of prosecutors would try to find a way to get those items into evidence. Penn wanted to try to get them in, but I intervened." He slid up in the chair and dropped his voice, which took on a conspiratorial tone. "You know," he said, "all I'd really need is a viable suspect. I assume you're doing your own thorough investigation. Have you come up with anyone you think might be a candidate?"

"I…well…we're looking at some different angles," I said.

"Because if you were to come up with someone solid, someone we could really pin this on in such a way that they'd have no way out, I'd have no compunction about dismissing the charge against Paul and refiling it against someone else. Do you know whether Miss Cartwright was into drugs?"

"I think she maybe smoked a little marijuana, but that's all we've discovered so far. Didn't your guys investigate Kasey thoroughly?"

"To be honest, and this is just between you and me and that plastic plant over there, I don't think Bill was as thorough as he could have been. He locked onto Paul pretty quickly and didn't let go until he had his indictment. Once he got the indictment, well, you know how it is. Once they're indicted and arrested, the cops turn everything over to the lawyers."

"So what you're telling me is that there's a chance that Kasey may have had a drug problem and may have gotten herself killed by a dealer? Why, because she owed him money?"

"It's certainly possible, isn't it?"

"I don't know. *Is* it?"

Johnson stood, walked to the window, and gazed out into the blue sky above the river.

"Let's just say you develop reliable evidence that Kasey had a drug problem," he said. "I'd think you could do that through some of her old classmates, some of the ones who need money. Then perhaps through some extremely diligent work on the part of your investigators, you happen to develop the name of a Nashville drug dealer who was selling to Kasey. I might even be able to help you with the dealer's name. Lord knows there are a lot of them out there on the street. Then maybe some previously unidentified hair and fiber evidence gathered from Kasey's room is connected to this drug dealer through DNA analysis. If those things were to happen, we could have an entirely new ballgame on our hands. Entirely new. And no one but you and I would ever know the difference."

I sat there, stunned, not knowing what to say. After a few seconds, I said, "Have you discussed this with Mr. Milius?"

"Wouldn't be prudent," Johnson said. "Man's got a murder charge hanging over his head. You never know who might be listening. I believe you can go ahead and leave now, Mr. Dillard. Please give what I've told you some serious thought, and be sure to tell Mr. Milius I said hello."

I got up and walked out of the room deep in thought. A district attorney had just told me how to fix my own case and offered to help me do it.

Now *that,* I thought, is a new one.

CHAPTER 28

As soon as I left the district attorney's office, I called Caroline and drove to Arnold's Country Kitchen on Eighth Avenue. I waited for Caroline in the parking lot, and about ten minutes later she showed up in a cab. She said she was feeling much better after the nap. We went inside the restaurant, which was housed in a garish, orange, concrete block building, and ate country food cafeteria style. It was good, too. I was glad to see Caroline load up her plate.

"So, the district attorney just offered to help me fix Paul Milius's case," I said to Caroline after we'd gone through the line and taken a seat in a corner near the door. "He says if I bribe some of Kasey's old schoolmates and get them to come to court and testify that she had a drug problem, he'll help me come up with a drug dealer here in Nashville and hang the murder around his neck. He even mentioned planting DNA evidence. Hell of a guy."

"Why would he do something like that?" Caroline asked as she slid a piece of roast beef into her mouth.

"I got the impression they're friends, but not the kind of friends you and I have. This is Nashville, Caroline. The state capitol. The seat of power and money in the state.

Friendship here means something entirely different than it means back home. I'm out of my league."

"You're not out of your league," she said. "What did you say to him?"

"Nothing, really. I didn't know what to say—I was so shocked."

"Should you call the FBI or something? Isn't that public corruption?"

"I suppose it was an attempt to commit a corrupt act, or at least a suggestion, but unless I follow through, nothing will come of it. And to answer your question, no, I'm not calling the FBI. I'd wind up being an informant for them, and that's one rabbit hole I never intend to go down."

"What about your client? Are you going to tell him?"

"Nope. I'm not saying a word."

"Do you think he's guilty?"

"Actually," I said with my mouth full of a roll, "I don't. I tend to believe Alex Pappas. I think Lana contracted the killing and wanted to kill Paul, too. I just can't prove it."

"It looks pretty bad for Paul, doesn't it?"

"It does, mainly because he's been such a man-whore. But they'll have trouble getting that kind of evidence in. These are two of the worst people I've ever dealt with, Caroline. Paul and Lana Milius are a real match made in hell. Both of them should probably be in prison. Lana for murder and Paul for stupidity."

"You'll win at trial," Caroline said. "You'll get the jury to see what's true and what isn't, and you'll win."

Caroline ate half the food on her plate and we walked outside to the car Lana had loaned us. As soon as she climbed into the passenger's seat, she took four huge pills—her new medication—out of a bottle in her purse and began taking them and washing them down with a cup of water she'd carried out of the restaurant.

"They said to be sure to take them with food," she said, "but they're so big they aren't going to leave much room in my stomach."

I'd scheduled a meeting at Charlie Story's office with Charlie, Jack, and Paul Milius. Caroline said she felt like she was losing touch with the case and wanted to sit in so we started in that direction, but less than five minutes after we pulled out of Arnold's parking lot, she started frantically telling me to pull over. I did, and she opened the door, stepped out, and started vomiting on the sidewalk. I got out of the car, walked around, and patted her back while she bent over and continued to wretch. It was so frustrating, being utterly unable to help her. We stood there for several minutes while cars whizzed by and people stared. A couple even honked their horns, probably thinking she was drunk. When she was finished, she got back into the car, wiped her mouth with a paper napkin she'd taken from the restaurant (just in case, she told me later), and announced that she wanted to go back to the hotel and lie down.

"I'm going to withdraw from this case," I said. "Lilly was right. I shouldn't have taken it in the first place."

"You'll do no such thing," Caroline said. "My husband does not quit just because things get a little tough."

"You're puking in the street, Caroline."

"So what? I've done it before."

"That was years ago when you first started the chemotherapy."

"This new medication is a form of chemo," she said. "Weren't you listening?"

"Yeah, I was listening, but what I heard was 'pill form' instead of intravenous, and I assumed the side effects wouldn't be that bad."

"You assumed wrong, and so did I. I have medication for nausea. I should have taken it before I ate. I'm sorry. I didn't mean to embarrass you."

"What? Are you kidding? After everything else we've been through, puking in the street is nothing. Piece of cake. You want to embarrass me, get naked and dance on the roof of the car while you're puking."

She reached over, squeezed my hand, and smiled. "Don't tempt me," she said. "And you're not withdrawing from anything. I mean it. I'll deal with this. I just have to get used to the new medication. Before you know it, I'll be as good as new."

CHAPTER 29

Charlie and Jack were waiting for me when I arrived at Charlie's office. Paul Milius hadn't yet shown up, which didn't really surprise me. Milius was turning out to be one of those clients who wanted to act like nothing was really going on. He was sticking his head in the sand and leaving pretty much everything up to us. Some clients wanted to be in the middle of everything; some wanted to control the investigation and the strategy and the tactics. They were, for the most part, both annoying and guilty. But others, like Milius, left it up to the lawyer. He didn't call, he didn't second-guess, and he didn't double-check. He just wanted to make believe his life hadn't changed at all. His attitude was, "Call me when it's over. In the meantime, leave me alone."

But we had to talk to him occasionally, so we'd set up this meeting. Charlie and Jack and I talked about Caroline for a little while—I didn't mention the little incident in the street—and then I spent some time filling them in on the details of my detour to Ecuador before Paul walked in just after two fifteen. He seemed angry and irritable.

"So where are we?" he said after we'd all settled into chairs around a table in Charlie's conference room. "The press is crucifying me, especially that crazy Nicole Gacy.

I'm on her show every night. Have you read the paper, watched television, listened to the radio? They have me tried and convicted. They've dug up every woman I've ever had a conversation with and are turning all of them into torrid sexual affairs. So please, tell me you're making some progress. Tell me you've found out who really killed Kasey and that this is going to end soon."

"It isn't going as well as I'd hoped, Paul," I said.

"What do you mean?"

"It just isn't going all that well, but we still have some time. Maybe something will come up."

"Like what?" Milius said. "Do you think someone is just going to come forward and raise their hand and say, 'Oh, I did it? You've got the wrong guy.'"

"That'd be nice," I said, thinking about the crooked offer Ronnie Johnson had made.

"So what have you been doing? What am I spending a million dollars on?"

"Time, Paul," I said. "You're spending your money on our time. And we're trying to use it to your best advantage."

"What have you been doing? Give me specifics."

I shrugged and looked at Jack and Charlie. "Who wants to start?" I asked.

"I'll go first," Jack said. "I've been spending my time interviewing people in and around the industry."

"I know," Paul interrupted. "It seems like somebody in my office gets a phone call every half hour wanting to know if it's okay to talk to you."

"I hope you're saying yes," Jack said.

Milius nodded. "Most of the time."

Jack picked a thick file up from his lap. "I've talked to twenty-six people so far," he said. "The consensus seems to be that you're a pretty good guy for the most part and an excellent businessman, but that you have a great deal of difficulty resisting the urge to…how should I say this? Seduce women. You're apparently some kind of sex addict."

"That isn't a crime," Milius said, shifting uneasily in his seat. "What else?"

"It might not be a crime, but it's damned sure a problem," I said, miffed that he would just blow off his indiscretions so lightly.

"How is it a problem?" he said. "You're a lawyer, supposedly a good one. You're not going to let the prosecution turn this into a trial about my sex life, are you?"

"It depends," I said honestly. "It depends on whether the prosecution can come up with any proof that you were having sex with Kasey—who was underage, by the way—and whether the judge says it's relevant."

"Then make sure they don't come up with anything, and if they do, make sure the judge doesn't let it in," Milius said.

"You don't 'make sure' a judge does anything," I said. "They do what they want. They have to follow the law, but sometimes it's a close call and they do what they want. And the appeals courts usually back them up. They protect their own."

"Bribe him."

"I'm going to pretend I didn't hear that," I said.

"I'm serious. I have millions and millions of dollars. Find a way to get to him."

"Listen, Paul. I don't bribe judges. I don't take part in fraudulent scams, I don't manufacture evidence, and I try very, very hard not to lie unless I absolutely have to. When I first met you, you told me you knew my record in court. I can try cases. I can't guarantee we'll win this one, but I can guarantee you I'll do the best I can, and I've had some good results in the past. I can also guarantee you that we won't cheat. If you want a lawyer that lies and cheats, go hire one. There are plenty of them out there. We'll go into court and tell the judge we can't get along and you want a new lawyer. He'll probably let you do it, and he'll probably give you some more time. But I'm keeping your million dollars. You and your wife both signed the contract that said the fee was nonrefundable, and after all the crap I've already had to put up with in this case, I'm not giving it back."

"Believe me, I've already looked around," Milius said. "I've talked to a lot of people about this, people with money and power, people whose opinion I trust."

"Yeah? And what do they tell you?"

"They tell me that the first thing about 99 percent of the lawyers out there will want to know is how much money I have. Once they find out, they'll figure out a way to spend just a little bit more than I have. So if I'm worth $400 million, which is about what I'm worth today but it's dropping by the hour, they'll figure out a way to bill for $400.1 million before everything is over. They'll scare the shit out of me by telling me I'm going to prison for the rest of my life if I don't do exactly as they say, then they'll delay the trial for years and gather huge piles of worthless information while they double- and triple-bill me every step of the way. Then, when it comes down to actually going to trial, they won't be any better at it than you are and I'll have a fifty-fifty shot at best."

"Sounds like you got some pretty good advice," I said.

"Yeah, so I'm going to stick with you, but I'm not paying you a dime beyond the million. If I get convicted, I'll still have the rest of my money when I get out in ten years. And I'm going to tell you again—all three of you— I. Did. Not. Kill. Kasey."

"Fair enough," I said. I almost admired him for a minute. Almost.

"What about you?" Milius said, looking at Charlie. "Have you been looking into my sex life, too?"

"It just seems to keep popping up," Charlie said. I watched her as an involuntary smile spread across her face. "Sorry about the pun," she said. "It wasn't intentional."

"Charlie has run down all the women who have borne your children," I said. "She's also talked to the prosecution's witnesses, at least the ones that would speak to her. She handled the independent DNA expert, too, and he says we can't legitimately challenge the match."

"Do you have any suspects?" Paul said.

I took a deep breath and let it out slowly. I wanted to tell him about Lana, but I was afraid of what he might do. Ricky Church's story had checked out, so he was off the suspect list. Cameron Jones had a rock-solid alibi. The estate manager, Oliver Payne, had turned out to be an overeducated, overpaid snit who spent most of his time jetting from Connecticut to Palm Beach to Franklin so that Paul and Lana wouldn't have to deal with pedestrian matters having to do with the management of their households. And I hadn't yet been able to get in to see Carl Browning.

"There are some possibilities," I said. "We'll let you know if we get anything solid. In the meantime, do you happen to know where Alex Pappas might have gone?"

"I don't have any idea," Milius said.

"His father is Greek, correct? Like you?"

"I'm not Greek. My family has been in this country for more than a hundred years. I'm as American as you are. But yeah, I think he mentioned something about his father being Greek. And his name is Alex Pappas. That's pretty Greek."

"What about his mother?"

"What about her?"

"Any idea where her family is from? He worked for you for three years. Did he ever mention his mother's family?"

"He might have, but if he did it went in one ear and out the other," Milius said. "I didn't hire him to chit-chat about his family. I hired him to help me keep everything organized, to do whatever I needed when I needed it done. We weren't friends. I was the boss and he was the employee. Why do you want to know about his mother, anyway?"

"Just trying to figure out where he might be."

"Why?"

"So we can talk to him and get him to trial if we need to."

"Alex barely knew Kasey, and he wasn't even around the night of the CMT show. He'd already split."

"But don't you find that coincidental?" I said. "Why would he and Tilly disappear just a couple weeks before Kasey was killed?"

"Because they didn't want to go to jail for stealing $200,000 of my money."

"You have proof of that?"

"I do. Lana has every receipt."

"Then why haven't you told the police about it?"

"Because I didn't want the press getting a hold of it. I was hoping they'd come back, and we could work out a way for them to pay back the money. We would have fired them both, of course, but I was hoping we could work something out without involving the police. Then Kasey got killed, and everything turned on its head."

I pushed myself away from the table, stood, and stretched, signaling that I was finished.

"That's it?" Milius said. "That's all you've got?"

"There are a lot of things you don't know, Paul. A lot of things you don't need to know and don't want to know. As the trial gets closer, there are going to be offers made, attempts at deals. There will also be some last-minute fireworks. It never fails. So my advice to you is to just let us handle it. Go about your daily routine, try to ignore the press, and don't say a word to anyone about this case. How are things going between you and Lana?"

"We're not talking. I moved all my things out of our bedroom into a spare down the hall."

"Try to placate her as much as you can. Don't antagonize her. I probably won't call her as a witness because if she says you've been a good husband, it opens the door for the prosecution to get into your sex life, but there's no point in risking that she's going to come in and testify that you told her you killed Kasey. You haven't done that, have you?"

"What? Told Lana I killed Kasey?"

"In a moment of weakness?"

"Of course not. I didn't kill Kasey, so I'm not going to confess to anyone that I did."

"Good. That's good. Stay in touch, and I'll see you again soon."

Milius got up and started toward the door, muttering under his breath.

"By the way, Paul," I said. "You're going to have to tell the jury what Kasey said to you. You're going to have to explain to them what made you so angry."

"Not gonna happen," he said.

"Yeah, it *is* gonna happen," I said. "You're going to have to tell them something, and it better be good."

After he'd walked out the door, Jack looked at me and said, "You just told him to lie."

"No, I didn't," I said.

"Yes, you did."

I turned to Charlie. "Did you hear me tell him to lie?" I said.

"Not exactly," she said. "Not in so many words, but—"

"I told him he's going to have to tell them something. That something could be the absolute truth."

"We're going to get hammered at trial, aren't we?" Jack said. "They're going to convict him and send him to prison."

"They might," I said, "but not without a scrap."

CHAPTER 30

I'd asked Charlie to check out Carl Browning and had been pleased with the results. Charlie had done an extremely thorough investigation, going so far as to find old classmates and two ex-wives. What she found was that Browning had been raised the son of a macho Navy pilot in Newport News, Virginia, but had grown up an asthmatic child, unable to do many of the things other kids his age were doing and overly protected by his mother.

Once he hit adolescence, though, the asthma symptoms disappeared, and Browning went at everything with a vengeance. By the time Browning entered the ninth grade, his father was attending the Naval War College in Newport, Rhode Island, and Browning was attending the prestigious Milton Academy in Milton, Massachusetts. He was a star in baseball and hockey, graduated from there at the top of his class, and went on to the University of Virginia, where he majored in political science and economics and graduated summa cum laude. From there, it was off to law school at Yale and then to a ten-year career as a political and military analyst with the Central Intelligence Agency.

He left the CIA in 2000, but none of the people Charlie talked to were able to tell him why. What they did say was that his relationship with his parents ended at the same time his career ended at the CIA. Browning spent a few months in New York City after he left the CIA and then, out of the blue, he left his wife and moved to Nashville and hooked up with an old law school buddy named Reed Cummings. Browning was given an immediate partnership in the law firm of Allen, Parks, Browning and Cummings, a firm that specialized in intellectual property law, entertainment law, and telecommunications law. He married a Nashville socialite late that same year, and two years after that began representing Lana Raines-Milius. I'd been trying to set up an appointment with him, but his secretary wouldn't do it without his approval, and he wasn't approving.

So I decided to call one last time.

"This is Joe Dillard," I said for the fifth time in six days. "I'm Paul Milius's attorney. May I speak to Carl Browning, please?"

"Hold, please," the faceless secretary said. She came back on the line a few minutes later. "May I ask why you would like to speak to Mr. Browning?" she said.

"You already know why I want to talk to him because I've told you FOUR FREAKIN' TIMES!"

"Please don't take that tone with me, sir."

"I'm in Nashville, and I'm going to come down there if you don't let me speak to him right now. I'm going to barge in. I'm going to make a scene. Somebody might get their ass kicked. Tell him that."

She was gone again, this time for a much shorter time.

"Please hold for Mr. Browning," she said, and the line clicked.

"Reduced to making threats, are we?" a snide, hostile voice said.

"Why the hell won't you talk to me?" I said. "I'm trying to investigate a murder case that involves the husband of one of your most important clients, and you can't even give me a few minutes of your time?"

"I wasn't at the Plaza Hotel the night Miss Cartwright was murdered," Browning said. "I have witnessed absolutely nothing that would be of any value to anyone in this case. I have heard absolutely nothing that would be of any value to anyone in this case. I am not under subpoena, and I haven't been ordered by a judge to speak to you. Anything you might want to ask me about Mrs. Milius would be covered by attorney-client privilege. So we really have nothing to talk about."

"You're married, right?" I said.

"What? What kind of question is that?"

"Does your wife know about you and Lana?"

"I should inform you that our firm records the calls on these telephones," he said.

"Good. That's good. So if anybody listens to this, your partners will find out that you're having sex with a client, a married client. Partners tend to frown on that kind of thing because it creates conflicts of interest out the wazoo. But that isn't why I called. The main reason I called is to let you know that I'm onto you, Mr. Browning."

"Onto me? How frightening. I'm trembling in fear."

"You should be because I'm going to mess you up. I hate guys like you. I hate smug, morally bankrupt, big-city lawyers who think they can get away with anything."

"And exactly what do you think I got away with, Mr. Dillard?"

"You're trying to get away with murder, for starters. You set up Kasey Cartwright's murder, and you're going to try to hang it around Paul Milius's neck. I think you're going to steal as much of Paul's money as you can. I'm onto you, though. You'll be in prison before you know it."

I hung up the phone and smiled. The whole call was a shot in the dark, a bluff. I had no idea whether anything I said to him was true. But after the things both Michael Pillston and Alex Pappas had told me, I thought it was worth the shot. The guy would do something, and with a little luck, maybe he would make a mistake.

CHAPTER 31

Michael Pillston looked at his lover and tossed a mixing spoon down on the counter in disgust.

"I can't believe it," Michael said. "I forgot to buy cocoa when I was at the store. I can't make this dish without it, so I guess I'm going back down the mountain."

"No biggie," Lenny Brown, also a chef, said. "I'll ride with you."

Michael and Lenny had met at a seminar in Nashville back in the summer and had begun dating. It had gone quite well thus far. They had many common interests—not the least of which was cooking—and their temperaments seemed to be well suited for each other. Michael was a bit more aggressive, Lenny a bit more passive, but they were both romantics, and they adored classical music. Michael was an excellent cellist and Lenny was an orchestra-caliber flutist. Their idea of a perfect evening was to cook a nice meal, drink a couple glasses of wine, and then play music together.

And tonight was to be another perfect evening. It was Valentine's Day, a Friday, their first together, and they were spending it in a chalet on Campbell Loop Road in the Smoky Mountains near Gatlinburg. They were planning a meal of porterhouse steak with red peppercorn jus, a fennel and radicchio salad with lemony olive vinai-grette, horseradish mashed potatoes, roasted mushroom with spicy breadcrumbs, and a triple-chocolate tart. They were planning to wash all of this down with a couple bottles of Silver Oak Cabernet Sauvignon, and both of them were halfway through their first glass. Tomorrow, they would get up around ten, prepare and eat a leisurely brunch, and then spend the afternoon skiing.

"It's still snowing," Michael said as he looked out the kitchen window. "Not as hard as it was, but it's still coming down."

"Thank goodness for all-wheel drive," Lenny said as he pulled his coat from the closet near the front door.

Michael did the same, and they went out into the breezy night and climbed into Michael's three-year-old Volkswagen. They didn't notice the battered, four-wheel drive pickup that was backed into an old logging road just up the street.

* * *

Carl Browning, attorney at law, was behind the wheel of the pickup. The truck belonged to Paul Milius's corporation and was used to take care of the livestock and tend the grounds at Xanadu. He had placed a GPS tracking device in Pillston's car two days earlier after Pillston had mentioned spending Valentine's Day in Gatlinburg to Lana. Browning had followed the couple to their Gatlinburg chalet earlier that day using the tracking device, and then he'd gone back down the mountain to a busy restaurant parking lot, where he'd quickly stolen a license

A CRIME OF PASSION

plate and attached it to the truck he was driving. Michael Pillston would die tonight. Browning had never killed anyone himself, but tonight that would change. Pillston was talking to Joe Dillard. Dillard said on the phone that Browning had "set up" Kasey Cartwright's murder and was framing Paul Milius. Lana said that information had to have come from Michael Pillston. Alex and Tilly were gone. It had to have been Michael. Dillard had interviewed him, and Michael was always lurking, Lana said, always listening and watching.

Browning had driven back up the mountain thinking he would wait for Michael Pillston and his lover to go to bed and then break into the chalet and shoot both of them with the .38-caliber pistol Lana had stolen from a drawer in Michael's bedside table, but now they were on the move, and another plan was forming in his head.

The snow earlier in the evening had left the roads in the mountains barely covered. It wasn't terribly slippery, but the roads were slicker than normal, and these roads were dangerous under the most benign conditions. They were narrow and wound through the mountains like tangled snakes, full of sharp curves, steep grades, even switchbacks. As Pillston's Volkswagen pulled onto the road and disappeared around a corner, Browning fired up the pickup, locked it into four-wheel drive, and pulled out of the logging road. He caught up to Pillston, who was driving slowly and carefully, in less than a minute. When Pillston pumped his brakes and slowed before a switchback, Browning pulled the wheel slightly to the left and hit the gas. His bumper struck the Volkswagen high on the trunk. The car spun off the road and disappeared immediately. Browning stopped the truck, got out, and walked over to the spot where Pillston went over the side. He could hear the car, still crashing through underbrush, trees, and rocks as he walked up, and then, as he looked over, it stopped, and he could see headlights several hundred feet below. Browning looked around and listened closely. He could see no other traffic, could hear no one coming.

He climbed back into the truck and headed back for Nashville, satisfied that no one in Pillston's car could have survived.

PART III

CHAPTER 32

The last eight weeks leading up to the trial of Paul Milius were torturous for me, largely because I felt so guilty about the death of Michael Pillston back on Valentine's Day. The news had reported that Pillston and his boyfriend, Lenny Brown, were killed in an accident. I'd asked Leon Bates to check with the sheriff in Sevier County, and Leon had done so. When he called me back, he said that it appeared Pillston and Brown had left their chalet while they were in the middle of cooking a meal, perhaps to go and get something they'd forgotten. Both men had low amounts of alcohol in their bloodstreams, and the police found two open bottles of wine in the chalet, but there was no alcohol in the car. The damage to the car had been catastrophic, as had been the damage to both Michael and Lenny's skeletal systems. It had been snowing; the roads were slick. It was dark. Everything led to the conclusion that they'd been killed in an accident, but I couldn't help feeling as though I was responsible after what I'd said to Carl Browning. I'd wanted a reaction from him, and I was afraid I'd gotten it. What was worse was that there was absolutely nothing I could do about it unless I wanted to kill Carl Browning. That, of course, was out of the question.

We kept digging, but as the trial date drew nearer, I became less and less optimistic. We had no real defense other than Paul's denial, and Paul was going to make a bad witness. I felt like we had to put him on the stand. I'd always believed that juries wanted to hear "I didn't do it" from the mouths of defendants, but some defendants were so unlikable that putting them on a witness stand was a huge risk. Paul Milius was one of those defendants. I could lead him through the direct examination and make him look presentable, but Pennington Frye, if he was worth a tinker's damn, would make him look terrible on cross-examination. He'd paint him as a money-grubbing, power-hungry schmuck, and that's pretty much what he was. Frye would also hammer him about being in Kasey's room that night. I could try to rehabilitate him in front of the jury as best I could, but I wasn't confident about it.

We also had no other suspects besides Lana, and I couldn't use anything Alex Pappas or Tilly Hart had told me without having them sitting on the witness stand in front of the jury. Jack and Charlie had run down every contact we could find for both of them, and we'd come up empty. I'd even paid a Spanish-speaking, former FBI agent $50,000 to nose around Ecuador for two weeks, and all he came back with was a nice tan and a long sigh.

On the other hand, the prosecution hadn't had any luck coming up with any admissible evidence of the affair between Paul Milius and Kasey Cartwright. I didn't know whether Ronnie Johnson had run interference, whether the country music artists who had knowledge of the affair had refused to talk to the police, or whether they simply hadn't tried all that hard. It had actually been a bit of a fluke that Jack had run across Derek Birch, and I doubted that Birch would have spoken to the police voluntarily, so maybe we were in the clear on that part of it. It wasn't a home run, but it left the prosecution without a clear motive.

The trial was due to start in a week, and we were in court dealing with last-minute matters, not the least of which was a motion *in limine* I'd filed. *In limine* is a Latin term meaning "at the start," or "on the threshold." A motion is just a request. My motion *in limine* requested that Judge Graves exclude any evidence relating to Paul Milius's sexual activities, including, but not limited to, extramarital affairs that had led to children born out of wedlock. I didn't want the prosecution parading a line of women onto the witness stand who would testify they had slept with Paul Milius. The primary argument in excluding the evidence was that its probative value was grossly outweighed by the prejudicial effect it would have on the jury, and there was plenty of case law to back me up. But Pennington Frye had filed a written response, arguing that any evidence he presented regarding Paul Milius's infidelities was evidence of his character, that his character was certainly relevant in a murder trial, and that the judge should allow him to call witnesses to prove infidelity.

"How many witnesses would you have, Mr. Frye?" Judge Graves asked after court was called to order and he had formally entered the written motion and response into the record.

"I could bring dozens," Frye said, "but I'm willing to cut it down to six if Mr. Dillard will stipulate in front of the jury that his client has cheated on his wife with at least twenty different women and has four children out of wedlock for whom he pays child support."

"Absolutely not," I said. "I won't stipulate a thing. None of it is relevant, Your Honor, and even if you found it to be relevant, it would be so prejudicial you'd have to exclude it. He's on trial for murder, not for adultery."

"But would you not agree that this adultery, especially in such excess, is evidence of his character?" the judge said.

"It might very well be," I said. "So he's a lousy husband and a womanizer. His libido is overactive, and his morals are questionable. That makes him a fine political prospect, but it doesn't make him a murderer. If they had some evidence that he was having an affair with the victim, it might be different because it might be used to prove motive in regards to jealousy or rage or rejection, but as far as I know, there isn't going to be any evidence presented of an affair between Mr. Milius and Miss Cartwright."

"Is that right, Mr. Frye?" the judge said, looking over his reading glasses. "Do you have any evidence that there was a romantic relationship or sexual relationship between the defendant and the victim?"

"There are certainly plenty of rumors," Frye said.

"Rumors are not admissible."

"I know that, Judge. It's frustrating because I'm convinced they were having an affair and that Miss Cartwright had broken it off not long before she was killed. But I don't have a tape or a video or an eyewitness."

"Then you're out of luck," Judge Graves said. "If the evidence you have of Mr. Milius's sexual misconduct could somehow be connected to the victim, then I'd let it in. But the fact that he's apparently been out chasing every skirt between Nashville and Timbuktu for the past several years isn't really relevant to this case, and like Mr. Dillard said, it would be highly, highly prejudicial. So I'm going to exclude any testimony, or even any mention, of Mr. Milius's adulterous conduct from the trial of this case. Am I clear on that, Mr. Frye?"

"Yes, your Honor."

"Mention it and I'll grant a mistrial immediately."

"I understand," Frye said.

I packed up my briefcase and headed toward the side exit that Pennington Frye had showed me back on the first day I'd come to court while the horde of media scrambled out of the courtroom behind me.

"Doesn't really matter that he excluded it," Frye said as we walked down a narrow back hall.

"Really? Why's that?" I said.

"These reporters will have it all over the news, all over Twitter, all over Facebook, all over the blogs in ten minutes," he said. "Everybody has a smart phone. There is absolutely no way you're going to get a clean jury pool."

CHAPTER 33

We spent two days picking a jury, the part of trial work I'd always found most grueling. When we were finished, we had eight men and four women, which I considered a victory. There were two African Americans (one woman and one man), one Mexican American man, and nine Caucasian Americans (three woman and six men.) They ranged in age from twenty-six to sixty-two, and they were a fairly intelligent group, which I also considered a victory. Prosecutors were notorious for dumbing down juries, for looking for simpletons with the hang-'em-high syndrome. I thought this group would at least listen to what I had to say, but as I'd learned over and over during my career as a trial lawyer—you just never, ever knew what a jury would do.

Prior to jury selection, Judge Graves had given a stern warning to everyone in the jury pool about using their cell phones during the selection process or the trial. He told them they would be sequestered, and he told them he would have their phones confiscated at the beginning of the trial and returned to them after the verdict. He also told them they would go straight to jail for contempt of court if any of them were caught even sniffing a smart phone while the trial was going on. I could see the changes in their faces while the judge talked to them. Some of them were visibly shocked, even terrified, at the idea of having to be without their phones for a few days. I even saw two women crying. And it made for some nice theater when the judge asked if anyone needed to be excused from jury duty. Dozens of them came up and made some of the lamest excuses I'd ever heard, ("I think my brain might be shrinking," was the best), but eventually, we managed to get it done.

After the clerk handed out buttons for the jurors to wear and a short break, Judge Graves told Pennington Frye to make his opening statement. Frye stood and straightened his tie. What follows is a boiled-down version of what he said:

"This is a simple case, ladies and gentlemen. Let me first set the stage. Paul Milius, the defendant, is the owner of Perseus Records, one of the most successful recording companies in the world. The victim, an eighteen-year-old country music artist named Kasey Cartwright, had been discovered by the defendant and had signed a record deal with his company. On the night of December tenth, there was a Country Music Television Awards show at the Bridgestone Arena in downtown Nashville. During that show, the defendant was seen arguing with Kasey Cartwright backstage. The argument became so heated that Miss Cartwright actually threw a full glass of iced tea into the defendant's face.

"After the show was over, both the defendant and Miss Cartwright went to an after-party at an upscale downtown restaurant. The victim left early and was taken by limousine to the Plaza Hotel downtown, where her record company had booked a room for her. A little later, the defendant had his driver drop him off in the parking lot of the Plaza Hotel. The defendant instructed his driver to go home and then walked up to Kasey Cartwright's room at approximately two in the morning. There is absolutely no doubt of that. The defendant was the last person to speak to Kasey Cartwright—the last person to see her alive.

"Kasey Cartwright was found dead in her room the following morning. An autopsy determined that she had been struck in the face and strangled, and a small piece of skin was found wedged between two of her teeth. That skin was removed and tested for DNA. The DNA test revealed that the skin wedged in Kasey Cartwright's teeth belonged to the defendant. He had a small wound on his hand consistent with the circumstances I just described to you. He has admitted being in the defendant's room. He has admitted to slapping her. But he says he didn't kill her.

"The proof might be simple, but it is irrefutable. Paul Milius became enraged at Kasey Cartwright, he slapped her, and he strangled her. It was a classic crime of passion, one that cost a promising young star—a beautiful, innocent young girl—her life. Once you've seen the proof, there will be no doubt in your minds, and you'll be comfortable in doing your duty, which will be to find this man guilty of second-degree murder."

* * *

And then it was my turn. I was uneasy for a lot of reasons, not the least of which was that my client was on trial for his life, or at least a significant part of it, and it was up to me to spin things in such a manner that the people sitting in the jury box would let him go home. They may not like him, they may not believe him, but I had to make them like *me* well enough that they would believe I would not lie to them, would not try to mislead them, and would not represent a man who was guilty. It was a slippery slope, one that I'd walked many times. If I lost my footing, I'd go sliding out of sight into oblivion, dragging my client, whom I still believed to be innocent of murder, along with me. And if that happened, even though I would eventually be able to crawl out of the abyss and return home to my life and my loved ones, Paul Milius would go directly to jail for a long, long time.

I approached the jury box, smiled, nodded deferentially, and began.

"This is one of those rare cases where the proof can be misleading," I said, "because almost everything that Mr. Frye said is true. My client, Paul Milius, one of the most respected men in the entertainment industry and a man who has never, ever been accused of any sort of crime prior to this, did go to Kasey Cartwright's room that evening. The proof will show that he went there to make up with her, to apologize for the misunderstanding they'd had earlier in the evening that culminated in Miss Cartwright tossing a glass of tea in Mr. Milius's face. But when Mr. Milius got to the room, Miss Cartwright was still angry, and she said something so hurtful that it caused Mr. Milius to slap her. Mr. Milius will tell you what she said when he testifies later in the trial. He regretted hitting her immediately and attempted to apologize, but Miss Cartwright ran into a bathroom and locked the door. Mr. Milius left immediately.

"The timeline, which is extremely important, is this: The hotel's surveillance tape will show that Mr. Milius entered through the lobby at two thirteen and entered the elevator on the first floor at two fifteen. The elevator took him directly to the thirty-first floor where he got off at two sixteen. There are no cameras outside the elevators on the individual floors, but we do know that Mr. Milius reentered the same elevator at two twenty-one and was out the front door of the hotel by two twenty-four. He was in the hotel for a grand total of eleven minutes. He called the Volunteer Cab Company at two twenty-five and was in a cab three minutes later.

"So if he killed her, he did it quickly, almost instantaneously. It would have had to have been premeditated, yet he isn't charged with first-degree murder. One can only speculate why. Perhaps the prosecution doesn't believe in its own case.

"Beyond this uncertainty, you will have to ask yourselves why a successful businessman with no criminal record would suddenly and without explanation murder a young lady who was making his record company tens of millions of dollars each year and who would have made much, much more in the years to come. Paul Milius had turned Kasey Cartwright into a star. He had discovered her and had provided her with access to some of the best people in the country music business. I'm talking about producers, sound engineers, musicians, backup singers, arrangers, songwriters, marketing people. You name it, Kasey had the best. If you look at the trends in the sales of her music, everything was up, up, up. No plateaus, no drops. There were nothing but good things in store for her.

"So the question becomes: If Paul Milius killed Kasey Cartwright, why did he do it? Our proof will show that he didn't kill her because he had no reason to kill her. You'll hear the prosecution say—in their closing argument, I'm sure—that they are not required to prove motive. That's true. Under the law, they're not required to prove motive. But in the court of common sense, people want to know why someone was killed, and in a case like this, there is no more important question.

"In the end, after you've heard all the witnesses and reviewed all the documents, after you've listened to what Mr. Frye has to say and what I have to say, there will be far more than a reasonable doubt in your minds as to whether Paul Milius committed this crime. There will be a mountain of doubt, and because of that, you will be required by law and by duty to find him not guilty."

CHAPTER 34

Judge Graves looked a bit hung over, but he seemed mentally sharp. He looked at Pennington Frye and said, "Is the prosecution ready?"

"Yes," Frye said.

The judge turned to me. "Is the defense ready?"

"We are."

Back to Frye: "Call your first witness."

Frye stood. "The state calls Maria Ortero."

A door at the back of the courtroom opened, and a young, slim, Mexican woman whose shoulders stooped slightly walked in. She was wearing black pants and a pink blouse, and she kept her eyes on the floor as she took short, quick steps down the center aisle of the packed but silent courtroom. She reached the witness stand, sat down, and the judge swore her in.

"Would you state your name please, ma'am?" Frye said.

"Maria Ortero."

"And where do you live, Ms. Ortero?"

"Here in Nashville, at 2250 North Jackson."

"How are you employed?"

"I clean rooms at the Plaza Hotel."

"Is that also here in Nashville?"

"Yes. It's downtown."

"Were you working on Friday, the eleventh of December last year, Ms. Ortero?"

"I was."

"Did anything unusual happen that morning?"

"I found a dead body."

Frye paused a few seconds for dramatic effect and scanned the jury. It was a bush-league ploy as far as I was concerned. Everybody in the room—pretty much everybody in the country—knew a murder trial was going on.

"In which room did you find this body?" Frye said.

"It was in room 3100, the Vanderbilt Suite. It's on the thirty-first floor, one of the nicest rooms in the hotel."

"And what time was it?"

"Around nine in the morning."

"Were you alone?"

"Elena Rodriguez was with me. We clean the suite together."

"Where exactly was the body located, Ms. Ortero?"

"She was on the bed in the master bedroom, lying on her back."

"So it was a woman?"

"Yes, well, a girl, really."

"About how old?"

"She looked young. Like a teenager. She was very beautiful. I didn't know it at the time, but I found out later she was eighteen years old."

I didn't object, although the statement was hearsay. It didn't matter. The jury had already heard she was eighteen during the State's opening statement, and they'd hear it a bunch more before the trial was over.

"What was she wearing?" Frye asked.

"A full-length, black dress."

"A formal dress?"

"I believe so. It looked like something you'd wear to a party if you were rich."

"Rich? Why do you say rich?"

"Because it looked expensive, and she was wearing a necklace that looked like it was made of expensive jewels, and there was a diamond bracelet on her wrist."

"Did you recognize this young woman?"

"No. I'd never seen her before."

"Did you notice any blood in the room?"

"There was blood on her lips. Not much, but some, and there were some scratches on her neck."

"Can you describe the position of the body on the bed for the jury, please?"

"Well, like I said, she was on her back, but she was lying across the bed about midway. Her feet were hanging off the side closest to the door, and her arms were spread straight out, palms up."

"Like Christ on the cross?"

"Objection," I said as I stood.

"Sustained. Knock it off, Mr. Frye," the judge said. Then he looked at the jury and said, "Ignore the reference to the Crucifixion."

Frye picked a photograph up off the table in front of him, held it up, and waved it. More drama.

"I'd like to show this photo to the witness and have her identify it," he said to the judge.

"Pass it to the bailiff."

A uniformed bailiff came off the wall to my right, took the photo from Frye's hand, and walked it to the witness stand. He handed it to Maria Ortero.

"Ms. Ortero," Frye said, "does the photo the bailiff just handed you accurately depict the position of the body the morning you walked into room 3100 at the Plaza Hotel at approximately nine o'clock on December eleventh of last year?"

She stared at the photo for a few seconds and looked up. "Yes."

"The State moves to admit the photo as Exhibit One," Frye said to the judge.

The judge looked at me. "Any objection, Mr. Dillard?"

"No, sir," I said. An objection would have been useless. It was certainly relevant, and it wasn't particularly inflammatory, unlike so many other death-scene photos I'd seen in the past. She almost looked serene. No real harm in showing it to the jury.

"So admitted," the judge said. "Show it to the jury."

The bailiff walked over to the jury box and handed the photo to the juror that occupied the far left chair in the first row of the jury box. We waited while the jury passed the photo from person to person.

Frye turned back to the witness. "What did you do after you discovered the body?"

"I…I didn't know what to do at first," Ms. Ortero said. "I moved closer and said, 'Miss? Miss?' That's when I noticed her coloring. Her face was pale, almost white. I called to Elena and she came right in. We both stood there looking at her for a little bit—I'm not sure how long—and then Elena said, 'She isn't breathing.' I thought about trying CPR on her, but the hotel discourages us from doing that kind of thing. I stepped over closer to the bed and reached down and touched her forehead, and she was cold, so very cold. Elena and I walked out of the room then, and I used my cell phone to call my supervisor."

Frye paused to let all of that sink into the jury's collective consciousness, and then he said, "Is there anything else you can think of that might help the jury, Ms. Ortero? Anything you may have seen or otherwise noticed?"

Maria Ortero shook her head.

"You have to answer," the judge said. "We can't record you shaking your head."

"No, nothing else," she said. "I thought it was just going to be another day at work. And now…well, now I'm here."

"That's all I have, Your Honor," Frye said, and he sat down.

I stood and walked to the lectern that was stationed directly between the defense table and the prosecution table. I smiled at the witness, but she was already shifting in the chair. She was nervous.

"How long have you worked for the hotel, Ms. Ortero?" I asked.

"A little over nine years."

"And how many days a week do you work?"

"Five, sometimes six."

"Always the same shift?"

"Yes. I work days."

"What time do you start and leave?"

"I get there at five in the morning and usually leave around two in the afternoon."

"Where do you enter the hotel, ma'am? Do you come through the front door of the hotel like the other customers, or is there an employee entrance?"

I heard Pennington Frye's chair slide. "Objection," he said. "I fail to see the relevance of this line of questioning."

"This is a murder trial, Your Honor, and it's cross-examination. I'm entitled to a little latitude."

"Objection is overruled. Continue, Mr. Dillard."

"Which entrance do you use when you come to work, Ms. Ortero?" I said.

"All the employees are supposed to use the service entrance."

"And where is the service entrance located?" I nodded to Charlie, who was sitting at the defense table with me. Charlie punched a few keys on her laptop, and a large architectural rendering of the building came up on an oversized monitor behind the judge as well as on half a dozen other monitors that had been placed around the courtroom for the trial.

"It's at the southwest corner of the building, near the kitchen," Ms. Ortero said.

Charlie clicked a mouse and a small area of the rendering lit up.

"Is that it?" I asked.

"Yes."

"Is there any security there?"

Ms. Ortero shook her head, prompting another rebuke from Judge Graves.

"No. No security."

"The employees don't have to go through any scanners, nobody checks their identification at the door, correct?"

"Correct."

"Is the service entrance door locked? Do you need a key or a card to get in?"

"No. No key or card. We just walk in."

"Are there security cameras at the entrance?"

"Not that I know of."

"So pretty much anyone can come in through that door, anytime, without being challenged or photographed?"

"Objection!" Frye said. "Calls for speculation."

"Sustained," the judge said.

"Thank you, Ms. Ortero, that's all I have."

CHAPTER 35

r. Joseph Pemberton was an expert in forensic pathology. I'd talked to Pemberton three times leading up to the trial and would have stipulated to his expertise in the field, but Pennington Frye was dying to impress the jury, so I sat there and continued to refine some points I wanted to make later in the trial while Frye droned on and on about Pemberton's qualifications. When he was finally finished and the judge had inevitably declared Dr. Pemberton to be an expert in his field, Frye finally got down to asking some pertinent questions.

"Dr. Pemberton, were you called on to perform an autopsy on the body of one Kasey Marie Cartwright back in December of last year?" Frye asked.

"I was."

"Would you outline the procedure and your findings for the jury, please?"

Pemberton began describing in great detail the incisions he made in Kasey Cartwright's skull and body, how her brain and tongue and internal organs were removed, examined, and weighed, and how tissue and blood samples were gathered and stored for testing that would be performed later. He said Kasey Cartwright hadn't had any alcohol to drink, and her drug screen was negative.

"There were contusions, some bruising, on the upper and lower lips about an inch to the left of the center line," he said, "with the center line being just beneath the center of the nose. The bruising is consistent with someone striking the victim with either an open hand or fist, most likely an open hand. The upper lip also had a small cut in it—about two centimeters in length—that appeared to have been caused when the lip was compressed between the victim's teeth and the attacker's hand. I found two small pieces of skin, one wedged between the lateral incisor and the bicuspid in the upper teeth and another wedged between the bicuspid and the first premolar in the lower teeth. Both pieces of skin were removed and stored separately for later analysis and identification."

"Ultimately, Dr. Pemberton," Frye said, "what were your findings as to the cause of this young lady's death?"

"She died from asphyxia due to manual strangulation," he said. "In layman's terms, she was throttled, or choked to death. Both her larynx and her hyoid bone had been fractured, and there was heavy bruising in the muscles of her neck. There were some finger-pad contusions visible on the neck, and there were scratch marks on the neck made by Miss Cartwright's fingernails."

"She scratched herself?" Frye asked.

"It's fairly common in manual strangulation cases," Pemberton said. "The victim reaches up to try to pull the attacker's hands from her throat, and she winds up scratching herself."

Pemberton also testified that the time of death was sometime between two and three in the morning, which was testimony I couldn't really challenge. So after a few more perfunctory questions from Frye, it was my turn. I stood at the lectern several feet from Dr. Pemberton. He was a studious-looking man, with serious gray eyes behind dark-framed glasses. He appeared to be around fifty, with short, salt-and-pepper hair, and wore a brown, tweed jacket. During my conversations with him leading up to the trial, I'd found him to be quite in awe of himself.

"Dr. Pemberton, just so the jury is clear on this point, you have absolutely no idea how Kasey Cartwright died, do you? And by that I mean you have no idea who killed her. You simply don't know, do you?"

The last thing an expert witness, and particularly a doctor, wants to hear from a defense lawyer is that he really doesn't know anything. Pemberton straightened in the witness chair, leaned forward toward the microphone, and said, "I know she was killed by another person and that she was strangled to death."

"But you have no idea who strangled her or why, do you?"

"I have my suspicions."

"Okay, you want to fence a little. Fine. You weren't there, were you? You weren't in the room that night?"

"Of course I wasn't."

"So you don't have any idea what happened, do you?"

"Like I said, I know an eighteen-year-old girl was strangled."

"Again, you don't know who strangled her, do you?"

"I know one of those small pieces of skin that was wedged between her teeth belonged to her, and the other belonged to your client, which means he struck her. It isn't much of a leap to conclude that he also choked her."

Bam! There it was for all the world, and the jury, to hear. The tiny piece of skin that was wedged between two of her lower teeth came from my client's right hand. It had already come up in the opening statements, and I knew it was going to come up later in the trial, most likely through the TBI criminalist or one of the detectives, but I wanted to start a fight so the jury would recognize early on that Paul Milius was being represented by someone who wasn't afraid of a fight. I hadn't been sure Pemberton would blurt it out the way he had, but I'd certainly hoped with a certain amount of goading that he would, and I'd been successful. Now that he'd done it, it was time for me to move on to the pissing match with the judge and the prosecutor. I needed to establish some turf and to let the jury know that despite what they had been brought up to believe about defendants' constitutional rights, despite the constant rhetoric about criminal defendants' rights being far, far too broad and courts too lenient, the fight in criminal court wasn't always a fair one. The media had already tried and convicted Paul Milius. The state had indicted him, and the state employed almost everyone in the courtroom, including the judge. I needed the jury to know that the judge and the prosecutor were willing to break their own rules, and that I wouldn't let them get away with it. I was sure the judge and the prosecutor thought I had committed a serious error by letting a little exchange with Pemberton blow up in my face, but one of the things I wanted to determine was whether the judge would do the right thing and rebuke the witness. He didn't, of course.

I paused for a few seconds before I said, "How many trials have you testified in, Dr. Pemberton?"

"This makes the fifty-fourth."

"Fifty-four trials. Then you must be familiar with the rules regarding hearsay evidence. At least you must have some working knowledge of what it is."

"I'm not quite sure what you're asking."

"You know someone can't come into court and tell the jury what somebody else told them, don't you?"

"I suppose I'm aware of some of the limit—"

"Yet you just threw the rules out the window and spouted off that little tidbit about the piece of skin you found."

"You walked right into it," the judge said. "You got what you deserved, Mr. Dillard."

"Thank you, Your Honor, for pointing out to the jury that you don't care about the rules of evidence any more than the State or its witness."

Before the judge could respond, I turned back to Dr. Pemberton. "You didn't test the piece of skin, did you, doctor?"

"I did not."

"Because that isn't your area of expertise, is it? You're a pathologist. You conduct autopsies and make conclusions regarding causes of death. DNA identification is not what you do, is it?"

"No."

"But since we're on the subject, who told you the piece of skin you found came from my client? The criminologist? The district attorney?"

Now Pennington Frye was on his feet. "Objection! He just chastised the witness for offering hearsay evidence, and now he's asking him for more!"

Things were going surprisingly well. I'd learned very quickly that I could create a fair amount of chaos with very little effort. Some defense lawyers call it "making the State come off their mountain to fight on my molehill." I just called it fun.

"That's enough!" Judge Graves said. "Approach. Both of you."

Frye and I walked up to the bench. Judge Graves's cheeks were pinker than usual, and Frye's back was a little stiffer than usual.

"Just what do you think you're doing, Mr. Dillard?"

"I'm cross-examining the medical examiner."

The judge's eyes narrowed. "I don't know how the judges run their courtrooms up there in the mountain country where you come from, but I—"

"They run them pretty much the same way you do, Judge. They help the prosecution every chance they get, and they treat defense lawyers like flies at a picnic."

"You're practically begging me to hold you in contempt."

"All I want is a fair shake. Level playing field. Same rules. All those clichés. Neither of you said a word when the witness blurted out hearsay. You probably thought it was funny. You even said I walked right into it. You want to try to hold me in contempt for being upset about it? Go ahead. All you'll do is delay the trial while I beat you in the court of appeals and then the case will get assigned to another judge."

His complexion had darkened from pink to almost purple, but he knew I had him, at least for now, and the jury knew I'd won, too, which was even more important.

"Move on to another line of questioning," the judge hissed. "Step back!"

I walked back to the lectern and faced Pemberton.

"So just to be clear, just so the members of this jury are clear, you don't know any more than I do about what happened in that room that night, do you, Doctor?"

"I know a young girl was strangled," he said meekly.

"Thank you. That's all I have."

CHAPTER 36

"**S**tate your name, please," Pennington Frye said.

"David Biggs."

"Where do you live, Mr. Biggs?"

"Outside Franklin, on the Milius estate."

"How are you employed?"

"I'm an assistant to Paul Milius. I help him with a lot of things, but the most important thing is to drive him from place to place."

"You're a chauffeur?"

"You can call it that if you like."

"Did you drive Mr. Milius anywhere on December tenth of last year? And I'm speaking of the evening in particular."

"I drove him to the Bridgestone Arena for the Country Music Television Awards show."

"What time did you arrive?"

"I think we got there around seven in the evening."

"And how long did you stay?"

"Mr. Milius came back out to the parking lot around midnight, I believe, and we left for the after-party."

"Did you witness anything that went on at the awards show?"

"No, I stayed near the car."

"Where was the after-party held?"

"Sambuca. It's a restaurant on Twelfth Avenue."

"How long did it take you to get from Bridgestone to Sambuca?"

"Not long. It's less than a mile, but there was some traffic. Maybe five, six minutes."

"So this is after midnight, and now it is December eleventh?"

"Correct."

"Did you go inside the restaurant, Mr. Biggs?"

"I stayed in the car and waited for Mr. Milius. I always stay with the car. It's a pretty boring job."

"How long did you wait?"

"About two hours, I guess."

"So it's now two in the morning, correct?"

"That's right."

"And did Mr. Milius come out alone?"

"He did."

"Where did you go from there?"

"Mr. Milius asked me to take him to the Plaza Hotel downtown."

"Did you do that?"

"Yes."

"What time did you arrive?"

"I'm not sure. It only took about five minutes to get there. Traffic was light. It was probably two ten, two fifteen."

"What happened when you got to the Plaza?"

"I dropped Mr. Milius near the front door. He got out and walked inside. Before he walked away, he told me not to wait for him, that he would see me in the morning at the usual time, and that I should go on back to Franklin and get some sleep. So that's what I did."

"Did you see Mr. Milius again that night?"

"No."

"When did you next see him?"

"At six thirty the next morning. I was waiting in the car for him when he came out of the house, and I drove him to work just like I always do."

"Any idea how he got home?"

"No."

"Did he say anything about the night before?"

"No."

"Does Mr. Milius often ask you to drop him off at hotels at two in the morning?"

"No."

"How many times would you estimate in the past that Mr. Milius has asked you to drop him off at a hotel at that time of night?"

"Never. That was the first time."

"And you've worked for him for how long?"

"Seven years now."

"That's all. Thank you, Mr. Biggs."

The judge looked down at me and said, "Any questions, Mr. Dillard?"

I stood up and thought for a second. Most lawyers cross-examine every witness, no matter what the witness said or didn't say on direct examination. Some do it because they're so anal retentive they simply have to dredge through everything again, others do it because they think they're not doing their job if they don't ask at least a *few* questions, and still others do it because they like to hear themselves talk. I'm of the opinion that if the witness hasn't hurt you too badly and really has nothing else to add, it's best to keep your mouth shut and sit down. David Biggs had testified that he dropped my client off at the Plaza around two in the morning. My client didn't intend to deny it. The only thing that really hurt—and it wasn't terrible—was that Paul Milius had never before asked David Biggs to drop him at a hotel at two in the morning. I decided to keep my mouth shut.

"No, sir," I said to the judge.

"Excellent. Mr. Frye, call your next witness."

CHAPTER 37

"My name is Donald Tuttle," said the man sitting in the witness chair. He was sixty, with thin, gray hair and wire-framed glasses. He was wearing a powder blue sport coat and a bow tie of the same color.

"What do you do for a living, Mr. Tuttle?" Pennington Frye said.

"I'm an insurance agent."

"Do you sell life insurance?"

"I do."

"And within the last year, did you sell a policy to insure the life of a young lady named Kasey Cartwright?"

"I did."

"To whom did you sell that policy?"

"To Paul Milius of Perseus Records, Incorporated. The corporation is actually the owner and beneficiary of the policy, but Mr. Milius contacted me on behalf of the corporation and signed the contract on behalf of the corporation."

"And how much was to be paid to Mr. Milius's company in the event of Miss Cartwright's death?"

"Thirty million dollars."

Frye held up a thick document.

"I'm holding a copy of the policy in my hand, Mr. Tuttle. Would you please identify it for the court?"

The bailiff handed the document to Tuttle, who examined it for a few minutes.

"Yes," Tuttle said. "This is the policy."

"So what you're holding in your hand there is a true and accurate reproduction of the original policy on Kasey Cartwright's life sold by you to Perseus Records, Incorporated?"

"It is."

"The state moves to admit the policy as an exhibit, Your Honor."

"So admitted."

"Thank you, Mr. Tuttle. No further questions."

I knew this was coming, of course, although I thought Frye might try to milk it a bit more. I don't think he really believed that Paul Milius killed Kasey Cartwright for insurance money, but it certainly did appear suspicious that the policy was taken out less than a year earlier, and $30 million was the kind of money that any juror would have to take into account when considering whether it was a factor in someone's death. I needed to deal with it.

"Mr. Tuttle," I said, "you're not just a run-of-the-mill insurance agent, are you? And by that I mean you're not the guy who tries to sell everyone in his church and civic club a policy. You're a big fish, aren't you? You make big deals."

Tuttle smiled slightly. I'd talked to him twice before the trial, had asked around about him, and had learned that he was amenable to flattery. I wanted him to be at least a little sympathetic to our side, so I fluffed him a bit in front of the jury.

"I've made some substantial sales, yes," Tuttle said.

"How long have you been in the business?" I asked.

"Twenty-two years."

"You deal primarily with businesses—big businesses—and you do a lot of what is known as 'key man' deals, isn't that right?"

"I see you've done your homework, Mr. Dillard. You're correct."

"And Kasey Cartwright is not the first country music star your company has insured, is she?"

"No. There have been several others."

"Including Lana Raines-Milius and a couple others who signed with Mr. Milius's record company?"

"Correct."

"And you basically value the artist by multiplying the artist's prior year's earnings for the record company by four, don't you?"

"That's typically the way it works, yes."

"So in Miss Cartwright's case, the fact that your company insured her life for $30 million meant that she earned eight million, or roughly eight million, the previous year for Perseus Records, Paul Milius's company?"

"Yes. I believe it was just over eight million, actually."

"And that would mean Kasey made how much? Around two million?"

"Objection!" Frye was on his feet, looking pained. "Mr. Dillard isn't a witness. He can't testify as to how much the record company grossed and the artist made."

"Why don't we ask the witness?" I said. "Mr. Tuttle, do you have firsthand knowledge of how the recording industry works?"

"Like I said, I've been in the insurance business for twenty-two years. I've sold key man insurance policies to more than three hundred recording artists, musicians, producers, promoters, and executives. Prior to becoming an insurance agent, I was actually a talent agent who represented the artists. I negotiated contracts on their behalf. That was exactly what led me to become an insurance agent because I realized I could make far more money selling the insurance policies. So, in answer to your question, yes, I have intimate, firsthand knowledge of how the industry works."

Frye sat back down, now looking a bit bewildered.

"All right," I said, "back to my first question. If Kasey Cartwright earned $2 million in the year preceding the purchase of the insurance, then did Mr. Milius's company gross roughly eight million from her work?"

"That would be about the industry standard," Tuttle said. "The recording artists typically wind up with around 20 percent of the gross."

"And were there plans to revisit Miss Cartwright's policy for the purpose of updating it anytime in the near future?"

"She was a rising star, Mr. Dillard. We would have gotten together once a year to update the amount of coverage. It would have increased."

"So if Paul Milius killed her, he cost himself a fortune."

"Objection!" Frye yelled.

"Sustained," the judge said sternly.

"Thank you, Mr. Tuttle," I said, and I suppressed a smile and sat down.

CHAPTER 38

"The State calls Lt. William Smiley," Pennington Frye said.

I'd spoken to Lt. Smiley a couple times leading up to the trial, once at Ronnie Johnson's office and another time at the police station downtown. He was stand-offish toward me, as many police officers are, because I was on the "other side." To him, I was a bad guy because I represented the interests of the person he had decided was the bad guy. His physical appearance reminded me a little of Jack in that he was dark-haired, dark-eyed, and strapping. He was ten years older than Jack, though, in his mid-thirties, and he walked confidently into the courtroom wearing a navy blue suit, a white button-down shirt, and a solid, navy blue tie.

The clerk swore Smiley in, and Pennington Frye spent a few minutes going over his background. They were trying to make it sound impressive, but I'd done my homework on Bill Smiley. Actually, Jack had done most of the homework. Jack had found a couple cops who were willing to talk to him about Smiley. He'd tracked down some of Smiley's old friends—including some old girlfriends—and he'd learned a great deal, not the least of which was that Smiley's position as a detective in the

Metro Nashville Police Department had as much to do with family ties (his father-in-law was an assistant chief) as it did his abilities. I couldn't use that information in cross-examination, but it always helped to know as much as possible about the witness with whom I was dealing.

Smiley's reputation, according to Jack, was that he was smart, but he was also lazy and he drank too much. He'd earned an associate's degree in business from a junior college and then switched to criminal justice at Middle Tennessee State University after he met the young woman who would eventually become his wife and whose father was a rising star in the Nashville PD. He got hired by the Metro Nashville PD right out of MTSU, spent two years on patrol and another doing undercover narcotics work before becoming the youngest homicide investigator in the department's history. He was a closet alcoholic—Jack said his sources told him Smiley drank Scotch whisky neat every day to the point of passing out—but he did his drinking at home and did his best to keep things on good terms with his wife, who was a registered nurse in the pediatric intensive care unit at Saint Thomas Midtown Hospital. They had no children.

Smiley had worked dozens of murders, both as a lead and assistant investigator. He'd been to half a dozen training programs around the country and was smooth and articulate in front of the jury. He avoided cop speak and, for the most part, talked like a normal human being. It was obvious he was an experienced witness.

"Would you please describe to the jury how you became involved in this particular case?" Frye asked.

Over the next half hour, Smiley described in detail how he came to be assigned to the case (he was up on the rotation), and the process he went through once he arrived at the hotel room. Cops don't exactly have checklists, but there are certain things that need to be done at every crime scene, and Smiley did them all. He secured the scene, he identified the victim, he took photos, he checked for blood and other evidence in all the rooms in the suite, (they found some blood that later turned out to be Kasey Cartwright's in the bathroom), he talked to Maria Ortero and Elena Rodriguez, the maids who found the body, etc., etc. He also documented everything he did in either field notes or reports.

"Tell the jury how you first developed Paul Milius as a suspect," Frye said.

"When I first walked into the room, I thought the victim looked familiar, but I wasn't certain who she was," Smiley said. "When I looked through her purse and saw her identification, I knew because I'm a big fan of country music. I wasn't all that familiar with Miss Cartwright's music, but I'd certainly heard the name and recognized the face after I made the connection. I knew she'd been on the Country Music Television Awards show the night before because I watched part of it at home. So after the initial identification, we started tracking people down, asking questions, conducting interviews. It wasn't long before we developed information from some of the CMT production people that indicated that the defendant and the victim had had some kind of disagreement during the awards show, so I managed to get in touch with Mr. Milius and asked him whether he would be willing to sit down and talk to me. He agreed and came downtown to our office. I read him his Miranda rights, and he signed a waiver and indicated he was willing to talk to me without having an attorney present, and that he was willing to sign a statement."

"Do you have a copy of the statement with you?" Frye asked.

"I do."

"Let's just cover the high points, and then you can pass it to the jury later," Frye said. "First of all, what did Mr. Milius say about the disagreement you referred to earlier? The one at the awards show."

"He said Miss Cartwright sang a song that she wasn't supposed to sing. Apparently she was supposed to sing a song that had been prearranged and agreed upon by everyone, and when she went on stage during the show, she announced to the audience that there had been a change in plans, and she sang a different song. Mr. Milius said he confronted her about it, they argued, and she wound up throwing a glass of iced tea in his face."

"Did he say it made him angry?" Frye asked.

"He said he was shocked for a minute, but not really angry. He went into a bathroom and dried off, and not too long afterward he left the awards show and rode to an after-party at Sambuca restaurant."

"And did Miss Cartwright also attend the after-party?"

"She did, according to Mr. Milius."

"So Mr. Milius told you she was there?"

"He did, but he said Miss Cartwright left early after Mr. Milius's wife insulted her."

"Insulted her?"

"He said his wife called Miss Cartwright a couple names. But he also said his wife was highly intoxicated and probably didn't even remember saying what she said."

"What time did Miss Cartwright leave the after-party?" Frye asked.

"Mr. Milius said she left around one fifteen, maybe a bit earlier."

"And what did Mr. Milius do after that?"

"He stayed at the party, which he said had become pretty subdued, until 2:00 a.m. Then he had his driver take him over to the Plaza Hotel and drop him by the front door. He told his driver he wasn't sure how long he would be, that he might even get a room, so he told the driver to go on home, and he went inside and took the elevator to the thirty-first floor. He said he loved Miss Cartwright like a daughter, and that he was terribly upset by both the incident at the awards show and by what his wife had said to her at the party. He said he wanted to apologize and to try to make sure everything was all right between them, both personally and professionally."

"So he admitted to you that he went to Miss Cartwright's room the night she was killed," Frye said.

"Yes. He said he knocked on the door and that Miss Cartwright answered a few minutes later. He said she let him in immediately and closed the door and that they were standing there talking when Miss Cartwright said something to him that infuriated him."

"What did she say?" Frye asked.

"He wouldn't tell me," Smiley said. "I asked him several times, but he flat refused to repeat what she'd said.

What he did say was that it made him so angry that he immediately snapped. That's how he put it. He said he snapped and he slapped her across the mouth before he realized what he was doing."

"And how did Miss Cartwright react?"

"He said she backed up a few steps and put her fingers to her mouth, and when she looked at them, there was blood. He said she started crying and turned and ran into the bathroom and locked the door. He said he went to the door and tried to apologize, tried to get her to open the door, but she was crying and yelling at him and cursing, and he was afraid someone would hear and that he might get in trouble so he left. He said he called a cab from his cell phone in the hotel parking lot and that one picked him up less than five minutes later. The cab drove him home to Franklin and he went to bed."

"Did Mr. Milius have any injuries when you spoke to him? And by the way, this was the same day Miss Cartwright's body was found, is that correct?"

"Yes. It was late in the evening, maybe seven o'clock, when he came to the office. And yes, he had a small cut at the base of the little finger on his right hand. I asked him about it, and he said he got it when he slapped Miss Cartwright. I asked him if he would be willing to provide us with a DNA sample and he agreed. We were notified the next morning by the coroner's office that they had recovered some skin samples from Miss Cartwright's teeth and that they had been preserved. We set up the testing and waited. It took a while, but when the test results came back, there was a DNA match between one of the pieces of skin in her teeth and Mr. Milius. We took everything we had to the Davidson County Grand Jury, they returned an indictment, and here we are."

"Thank you, Lieutenant," Frye said. "Please answer Mr. Dillard's questions."

I moved to the lectern and didn't hesitate.

"You certainly asked Mr. Milius whether he killed her, didn't you?" I said.

"Of course."

"And he denied it?"

"He did."

"How would you characterize his denial?"

"I'm not sure what you mean."

"How would you characterize it? Was it vehement? Was it flippant? Was it lukewarm?"

"Objection," Frye said. "He can't know what was in the witness's mind."

"I'm not asking him what was in the witness's mind," I said. "I'm asking him to vocalize an observation."

"Overruled," the judge said. "Answer the question."

"I'd have to say he was insistent," Smiley said. "That's probably the word I would use."

"So he kept insisting he didn't kill her? Is that accurate?"

"Yes. I'd say so."

"And he came voluntarily, correct? You didn't have to chase him down."

"He came voluntarily."

"Without a lawyer."

"That's right."

"He's a wealthy man, you know that, correct? He could afford a lawyer."

"I'm aware that he's wealthy."

"Yet he was more than willing to talk to you, correct?"

"He was willing."

"Because he said he wanted to tell you the truth, correct? He said he thought you might find out he was in Kasey Cartwright's room that night, and he didn't want you to get the wrong idea, isn't that right? He wanted you out looking for the real killer instead of focusing on him. Isn't that what he said?"

"I seem to recall something along those lines."

"But once you heard that he'd slapped her and once you heard there might be a DNA match with a piece of skin, you made up your mind, didn't you? You had your man."

"I think it was a logical conclusion," Smiley said. "He was there. He was the last person to see her alive. He admitted that he struck her. He admitted that he was angry when he slapped her. He said he snapped. That's the word he used. 'Snapped.' He called a cab at two thirty in the morning and had them drive him all the way to Franklin. The conduct is consistent with guilt, Mr. Dillard."

"In your opinion," I said.

"In my opinion."

"The only opinions that matter here are the ones that will be formed by those people sitting over there," I said, pointing at the jury. "And in order for them to develop an informed opinion, they need information. Who did you interview besides Mr. Milius?"

"Do you mean me, personally?"

"Yes. You. You interviewed Ms. Ortero and Ms. Rodriguez at the scene, correct?"

"That's right."

"And then some of your colleagues went out and did some interviews and developed information that led you to Mr. Milius, correct?"

"That's right."

"And then you interviewed Mr. Milius, right?"

"That's right."

"Who else?"

"I pretty much had what I—"

"What about Mr. Milius's wife? Did you talk to her?"

"One of my colleagues attempted to contact her and was told she did not want to speak to the police."

"Any follow-up?"

"Not that I know of."

"What about his staff? Do you know how many people work for him?"

"I don't."

"So you didn't talk to any of them, correct?"

"No need, Mr. Dillard. You're just trying to confuse the jury."

"I'm not trying to confuse anyone. I'm just pointing out that you didn't do much before you decided to charge this man with murder and put him on trial for his life."

"Objection! Argumentative!" Frye shouted.

"Sustained," the judge said.

"What about Mr. Milius's co-workers, employees, friends, associates? Talk to any of them? Yes or no."

"No."

"What about Kasey Cartwright's family? Talk to any of them?"

"No."

"None of her friends? Associates? Country artists who might have known her? People who were at the show or at the party that night?"

"Your client is powerful, like you said. He has money. None of the people who were at the show that night would talk to us. Neither would anyone at the after-party."

"I have to hand it to you, Mr. Smiley," I said, deliberately dropping his rank. "In all my years doing this, and there are more than I care to admit, you may have done the least thorough murder investigation of any police officer I've ever seen."

"Objection!" Frye said.

"Sustained."

"It was open-and-shut, Mr. Dillard," Smiley said, raising his voice. He was leaning forward now, his hands wrapped around the rail at the front of the witness stand. "Paul Milius was angry, he went to Miss Cartwright's room, he became even angrier, he slapped her, he strangled her, and he ran away."

"Why?" I said, raising my voice to meet his. "She was making him millions a year and would have continued to do so for years to come. Do you really think he killed her because she doused him with a glass of tea?"

"It isn't my job to prove why he killed her," Smiley said. "Just that he killed her."

"Well, sir, you failed miserably," I said. "On both counts."

I turned indignantly away and sat down next to Charlie.

CHAPTER 39

We were four days into the trial and the prosecution was about to rest its case. Everyone around me— Jack, Charlie, Caroline when I talked to her on the phone at night—said it appeared I was holding my own. The talking heads on television were saying a lot about the prosecution's inability to prove motive, and they were saying the lack of a motive could give rise to reasonable doubt in the jurors' minds. I felt like I'd developed a pretty good rapport with the jury, but I was, as always, uneasy. I still had a lot to overcome and a long way to go.

"Is there anything we need to take up before I call the jury in?" Judge Graves asked before the afternoon session began.

"Yes, Your Honor," Pennington Frye said. "We have a new witness, someone that was not on our list, and we'd like to call her first."

"Who is the witness?" the judge asked.

"Lana Raines-Milius."

I stood, stunned, while the gallery behind me erupted in a collective gasp. Lana had been conspicuously absent from the courtroom. She'd pretty much fallen off the face of the earth as far as I was concerned, but I was okay with it. I didn't want her around because I knew she was capable of almost anything. Paul had told me that he and his wife had been staying at arm's length, observing an uneasy truce in the false paradise that was Xanadu. He certainly hadn't mentioned anything about her popping up as a witness for the prosecution.

"This is dangerous territory," I said, trying to think. "I object. I have no idea what she's going to say. I haven't had any time to prepare any kind of cross-examination. And like Mr. Frye said, she wasn't on the list. This could be highly prejudicial."

"What is she going to say, Mr. Frye?" the judge asked.

"First of all, let me say that prior to last night, Mrs. Milius had steadfastly refused to speak to the police or to anyone in our office about this case, and to be frank, we didn't push it, primarily because of spousal privilege. But she called yesterday evening and wanted to talk—"

"*What is she going to say?*" Judge Graves said again, irritation in his voice.

"She's going to say that Mr. Milius admitted to her that he strangled Miss Cartwright."

"Outrageous," I said. "I've talked to her several times, and she's never said anything remotely similar. Besides that, if it happened, it's hearsay, it's unreliable, and it's a private communication between a husband and a wife. It's privileged."

I knew that everything I'd just said was wrong. The statement wasn't hearsay because it was an admission against interest, which is an exception to the hearsay rule. I couldn't prove the statement wasn't reliable, and the spousal privilege probably wouldn't apply. There was plenty of law on the subject, and courts consistently held the privilege didn't apply when people admitted to their spouses that they'd committed a murder.

"You say Mrs. Milius only came to you last night?" the judge said.

"That's right. I have a couple witnesses, investigators from our office, who can come in and verify that under oath if you'd like."

"Not necessary," the judge said. "I don't doubt your word, Mr. Frye. Why did she wait so long?"

"She said she was threatened. You'll understand when you hear her testimony."

"When did Mr. Milius make this alleged confession?" the judge asked.

"The night he was first questioned by the police," Frye said. "I'll be sure to get all the details out on direct, and if I miss anything, I'm sure Mr. Dillard will cover it on cross."

"Your Honor, this will be beyond prejudicial," I said. "And for the record, my client asserts the marital privilege. He objects to his wife repeating anything he said."

"I suppose it *will* be prejudicial, Mr. Dillard," the judge said. "If I let her testify. Where is she, Mr. Frye?"

"Down the hall in my office."

"Send someone to get her."

A couple minutes later, Lana walked in through a side door. She was wearing clothing more appropriate for a lawyer than a country music star, a charcoal gray skirt and jacket with a black blouse. Her face and hair were done perfectly. She strode past the defense table without looking at me and went straight to the witness stand. I turned and looked at Paul. "No matter what she says or what the judge does, don't react," I said. "Just let me handle it."

"Step up and take a seat," the judge said, and he had the bailiff swear her in.

"What is your name, please?" Judge Graves said.

"Lana Raines-Milius."

"Mr. Frye, the prosecutor for the State of Tennessee, tells me that you wish to testify in this case," the judge said. "Your husband is on trial for murder, and you wish to give testimony that could benefit the State of Tennessee and harm your husband, is that correct?"

"Yes."

For the next fifteen minutes, the judge questioned Lana about the circumstances under which Paul supposedly admitted that he killed Kasey. It was even worse than I thought it might be. When he was finished questioning her, he looked at me and said, "I can't see any good reason why she shouldn't be allowed to testify. You can cross-examine her about why she held back for so long, Mr. Dillard. As a matter of fact, you can cross-examine her about almost anything. I'll give you plenty of leeway. I'll even give you a little time to prepare after Mr. Frye is finished with her. But as far as the marital privilege, I'm going to rule that it doesn't apply."

"I suppose there's nothing I can do right now if you've made up your mind," I said. "But if my client gets convicted, it'll certainly be an issue."

"Appeal to your heart's content, Mr. Dillard," the judge said. He turned to the bailiff and said, "Bring in the jury."

The jurors filed in with Lana sitting on the stand. Once they were settled, the judge said, "Ladies and gentlemen, we had a short hearing about some legal matters while you were out. This lady sitting in the witness chair is named Lana Raines-Milius. She has already been sworn in and is about to testify." He looked at Frye and said, "Go ahead."

"State your name for the jury, please," Frye said.

"Lana Raines-Milius."

"And where do you live, Mrs. Milius?"

"I live in Franklin on an estate called Xanadu."

"What is your relationship to the defendant, Paul Milius?"

"I'm his wife."

"How long have the two of you been married?" Frye asked.

"Since I was eighteen. Fifteen years now."

"Mrs. Milius, are you here testifying voluntarily? Has anyone forced you?"

"No one forced me. I'm here because I think it's the right thing to do."

"Mrs. Milius, back on December tenth of last year, did you attend the Country Music Television Awards show with your husband?"

"I went to the show and Paul was there, but we arrived separately and we left separately. We didn't get along very well that night," Lana said. "Actually we haven't gotten along very well for quite some time."

"And why is that?"

"Objection!" I said, and I stood immediately. "Sidebar, Your Honor?"

Judge Graves waved us up and said, "Keep your voices down, both of you. State the grounds for your objection, Mr. Dillard."

"The question is designed to elicit testimony regarding Mr. Milius's extramarital affairs. She's going to say they haven't gotten along because he can't keep it in his pants or something along those lines. You've already ruled that kind of testimony inadmissible."

"Mr. Frye?" the judge said.

"I have no idea what her answer will be," Frye said. I wanted to kick him in the shin because he was obviously lying.

"If she mentions other women, I'm going to ask for a mistrial," I said.

"Step back," the judge said, and Frye and I returned to our tables. "The objection is sustained, the question is withdrawn. Mrs. Milius, do not answer the question Mr. Frye just asked you. Mr. Frye, move along to something else."

"Did you witness an argument between your husband and Kasey Cartwright that night?" Frye said.

"I saw her throw a glass of tea into his face, if that's what you're talking about."

"What time did you leave the show at the Bridgestone Arena that night?"

"Around midnight, the same as everyone else."

"And where did you go from there?"

"To the Sambuca restaurant where Paul was hosting an after-party for some of his company's employees."

"Did anything unusual happen at Sambuca?"

"I called Kasey a cow and told her she didn't have any talent, and Paul wound up calling my driver to come and pick me up and take me home."

"What time was that?" Frye asked.

"I'm not sure. I'd had too much to drink, but I think my driver, Bennett, probably got there around one forty-five or so," Lana said.

"And you went back home?"

"Yes. Went home and went straight to bed."

"When was the next time you saw your husband?"

"I saw him when he came in from talking to the police the following night. It was probably around nine thirty, ten o'clock."

"What was his demeanor? Did he seem normal?"

"He was scared," Lana said. "He was fidgety and was pacing around the bedroom. He told me he'd been at the police station, that someone had killed Kasey and that he felt like the cops were trying to pin it on him. He said it so nonchalantly, though, the part about Kasey, like it didn't matter that she was dead, just that they were trying to pin it on him. I mean, I almost fainted when he said she was dead. We weren't close or anything, but just the night before I'd seen her singing live in front of that huge audience at Bridgestone, and then I'd been sitting right across the table from her at the restaurant. It was surreal to think that she was dead. But Paul just kept harping about some detective named Smiley and how he was so smug.

"And then he let it slip that he'd actually been in Kasey's room after the party. And I looked at him and I said, 'Paul, you went to her room?' And he said, 'Yes. I went to her room. Not only did I go to her room, I *slapped* her, Lana. I actually slapped her in the mouth.' And I said, 'Why did you slap her?' And he said, 'Because she was an ungrateful little bitch. She wanted to change labels. Can you believe that? After everything I'd done for her, she wanted to just leave and go to another label. It made me so mad I popped her right in the mouth, which is how I cut my finger right here, which means the police are probably going to come up with some kind of blood evidence or DNA or something.' I said, 'Paul, did you do this? Because if you did, we need to start figuring some things out. You need to get a lawyer.' And he said, 'No, no lawyer. That just makes me look guilty.' So I said, 'Are you? Did you kill that girl?' And he just looked down and said, 'It happened so fast. It was like a dream, like I was watching myself but I couldn't stop myself.' He said he grabbed her by the throat and just started choking the life out of her, and the next thing he knew she wasn't breathing. He said they were standing next to the bed, so he just laid her down on the bed and walked out of the room. And then he said, 'She deserved it, Lana. I swear to God she deserved it. If it hadn't been for me, she would have been on her way to a junior college. I made her a star.'"

"Just so the jury is clear," Frye said, "when did he tell you all of this?"

"That night. It was the same day they found her body, that night after he came home from talking to the police."

"This would have been four full months ago," Frye said. "Why have you waited so long to come forward?"

At this point, Lana broke into tears. She was so convincing that I found myself thinking she should have taken up acting instead of singing.

"Paul is a very, very rich man," Lana sobbed. "After he told me, I think he regretted that he'd done it, and he said if I repeated a word of it to anyone, he would hire someone to kidnap and kill me and dump my body where it would never be found. I've been terrified ever since, but I've decided that I just can't live with Kasey's death on my conscience, even if he can. I have a fair amount of money myself. I'll go into hiding if I have to."

And then, for the *coup de grace*, she looked directly at Paul, leaned forward, and shouted, "I'm not afraid of you anymore, Paul! Do you hear me? I'm not afraid of you anymore!"

CHAPTER 40

The judge gave me thirty minutes to prepare for my cross-examination of Lana Milius, but I didn't think it would matter. I felt like we were pretty much dead in the water. If I went at her too hard, I might come off looking pathetic and desperate, but if I went at her too softly it could appear as though I thought she might be telling the truth. In all my years of practicing law, I'd never had a surprise witness inflict such devastation on one of my clients. Jack, Charlie, Paul, and I were sitting in a small anteroom about thirty feet down the hall from the jury room. Paul had ranted for ten minutes about his lying bitch wife, but other than that, we hadn't really said much. Finally, I stood, and Jack said, "What are you going to do, Dad?"

"I'm going to get her on her heels and try to keep her there. I'll just give her hell and hope for the best."

We walked back into the courtroom and took our seats at the defense table. Pennington Frye and his crew walked in a few minutes later. The gallery was packed, as it had been for the entire week. Judge Graves and his clerk entered about five minutes after Frye.

"Bring the witness back in," the judge said to the bailiff, and Lana reappeared shortly thereafter.

"Bring the jury back in."

The jurors filed in and took their seats.

"Mrs. Milius, I'll remind you that you're still under oath," the judge said. "Mr. Dillard, you may cross-examine the witness."

I stood up and looked at Lana. She was staring back at me, a look of defiance in her eyes.

"So your husband told you he went to Kasey's room, they argued about her switching record labels, he slapped her, and then he strangled her, correct?"

"That's what he said."

"And he told you all of this the day after it happened, so it was fresh in his mind."

"I suppose it must have been," she said.

"There's a problem with it, though," I said. "Wait, let me rephrase that. There are a million problems with it, but one that jumps out at me immediately is that what he told you doesn't work with what the police found at the scene."

"I beg your pardon?"

"You said he told you they argued, he slapped her, and then he strangled her. He said it happened very quickly, according to you. But what about the blood in the bathroom?"

"I have no idea what you're talking about," Lana said.

"Of course you don't because you're lying. The police found traces of Kasey's blood in the bathroom sink where she cleaned up after Paul admittedly slapped her. You left that part out. Did you forget or are you lying?"

"I don't know anything about any blood in any bathroom," Lana said. "All I know is what Paul told me, and what he told me is what I testified to a little while ago."

"So you're saying Paul lied to you?"

Lana looked confused for a second. I'd managed to do what I wanted. She was on her heels, at least momentarily.

"He might have."

"He might have? He might have lied to you about strangling Kasey? Why would he do that?"

"He didn't lie to me about strangling Kasey, Mr. Dillard. He admitted it right there in our bedroom."

"Are you saying he admitted to a false version of what may or may not have happened in that room that night?"

"I don't know what version he admitted to. He's a practiced liar, Mr. Dillard. You know the old saying, 'If his lips are moving, he's lying'? That's Paul."

"Yet you've been married to him for fifteen years."

"Yes. Fifteen miserable years."

"I'm sure we all feel terribly sorry for you, Mrs. Milius. What do you have, fifteen, sixteen servants out there on your thousand-acre estate? Your very own private jet? You're worth close to $200 million on your own, aren't you?"

"Objection," Frye said. "Relevance."

"Overruled," Judge Graves said. "I told you I was going give him plenty of latitude."

"Aren't you, Mrs. Milius? Worth close to $200 million?"

"I suppose it's somewhere in that neighborhood."

"And that's *your* money. Not his. Yours."

"Do you have a point, Mr. Dillard?" Lana said.

"The point is if you've been so miserable, why not just leave? You can certainly afford it. Why not just pack up and hit the road? Go someplace else?"

"I have no intention of leaving," Lana said, her voice becoming more intense, a bit shriller. "Xanadu is my home. It's mine. He spends hardly any time there. He's usually off gallivanting around the world or shacking up with some little whore."

"Wait a minute, Mrs. Milius," I said. "Wait just one second. That isn't what you told me at all. You told me your husband is impotent. Remember that? At the restaurant the first night we met? You told me he was impotent, didn't you?"

"I said no such thing."

"But if you did, you were lying, correct? Just like you're lying now."

"I said no such thing. You're just trying to twist things around and make me look bad."

"You're doing a fine job of that all by yourself," I said. "What happened to your personal assistant, Mrs. Milius?"

"My what? Why, she's in the building somewhere, I believe."

"I'm talking about your first cousin, Tilly Hart, the young woman who was your personal assistant for almost fifteen years but who disappeared back in November, just a short time before Kasey Cartwright was killed?"

Lana turned to Judge Graves and said, "Why are you letting him dredge up this sort of thing?"

"You wanted to testify," Judge Graves said. "This is what you get."

"What happened to your first cousin and personal assistant, Mrs. Milius? Tilly Hart. What happened to her?"

"I have no idea."

"She disappeared, didn't she? Along with Paul's personal assistant, a young man named Alex Pappas?"

"They stole from us," Lana said.

"Stole from *us*? From you and Paul? What did they steal?"

"They used a credit card of Paul's to buy things. Two hundred thousand dollars' worth of items."

"And you discovered this theft? You personally?"

"I did."

"And you called the police immediately, correct?"

"Nobody called the police."

"Two hundred thousand dollars and nobody called the police? That's because nobody stole anything from either you or Paul, isn't that right, Mrs. Milius? In fact, that entire allegation was a ruse so that you could apply pressure to Alex Pappas to get him to do what you wanted him to do, isn't that right?"

"Now you're being absurd, Mr. Dillard."

"Am I?" I decided to go for it and let my voice get louder. "Let's see if we can't bypass absurd and go straight for obtuse, then, shall we? You blackmailed Alex Pappas into hiring a contract killer to murder Kasey Cartwright and your husband because you thought Kasey and your husband were having an affair, isn't that right?"

"That's the most ridiculous thing I've ever heard," Lana said, her voice rising to meet mine.

"Your Honor," Frye said over her, "don't you think this is getting out of hand?"

"But something went wrong that night and only Kasey was killed." I was almost shouting now. "Isn't that right, Mrs. Milius? And now you're in here lying about what you say your husband told you so you can send him off to prison! Isn't that right, Mrs. Milius? You're lying, aren't you? Your personal assistant and your husband's personal assistant both disappeared on the same day, didn't they?"

"Your Honor!" Frye was shouting, too.

The wooden gavel banged and banged and banged.

"That's enough!" Judge Graves said. "Enough!"

He glared down at me, then at Frye, then back to me. He looked over to the bailiff and jerked his head toward the jury.

"Take them out of here," the judge said. As soon as they were out of the courtroom, he looked back at me and said, "Mr. Dillard, I told you I'd give you some latitude, but I'm not going to let you turn my courtroom into a circus."

Too late, I thought, but I kept my mouth shut and stared back at him.

"Do you have any proof, anything you're going to offer in your case, regarding the allegations of contract killing that you just made against Mrs. Milius?"

"I have no intention of revealing our case to either you or the prosecution at this point in the trial," I said.

"Don't!" Judge Graves said. "Don't test me, Mr. Dillard."

"All I can tell you is that I had a good-faith basis for the questions," I said. "I was afforded an opportunity to talk to Alex Pappas and Tilly Hart while I prepared for the trial. Alex told me Mrs. Milius forced him to set up a contract killing. He said she falsified credit card receipts, forged his name, and made it look like he'd stolen $200,000. Beyond that, he and Miss Hart were in a romantic relationship, and Miss Hart's life was threatened. He said he emailed information to the contractor and wire-transferred money to an offshore account and that Mrs. Milius was with him when he did it."

"Why in God's name isn't he here to testify then?" the judge said.

"He's in a foreign country. I honestly don't know where he is now. What I do know is that both he and Miss Hart are terrified of Mrs. Milius. I also know Alex is afraid he would be prosecuted for his involvement in Miss Cartwright's murder."

Judge Graves shook his head slowly.

"What a mess," he said. "In all my years on the bench, I've never seen or heard anything like this. I don't have any idea exactly what's going on here, but I think it's gone far enough. Mrs. Milius, you're excused."

Lana looked at him, confused.

"You're excused," the judge said. "You're done testifying in this case. I'll instruct the jury to make no inference from your absence when they return, but your testimony in this case has come to an end."

Lana stood and straightened her skirt. Then she gave me a look that made me remember what Tilly Hart had said in Ecuador: "Be careful, Mr. Dillard. She'll kill you if she thinks she needs to. Don't doubt that for one minute."

CHAPTER 41

Pennington Frye rested his case after the judge told the jury that they could believe all, part, or none of Lana Milius's testimony, and they should make no inference as to her being excused. I didn't know quite what to make of everything, but I felt as though I'd done a pretty good job of attacking Lana's credibility in front of the jury. The fact that the judge had given her the boot would have to make at least some of the jurors question what she'd said.

Once Frye rested his case, Judge Graves excused everyone until the following morning. As soon as I left the courtroom, I drove to the house where I was staying in Belle Meade. I didn't want to stay in a hotel because they were full of reporters, I didn't want to stay with Jack or Charlie because I didn't want to be a problem for either of them, and I certainly couldn't stay at Xanadu, so Caroline had helped me find a nice, privately owned, two-story house in Belle Meade that I could rent by the week. I drove there after court, took a short nap, talked to Caroline on my cell for about half an hour, took a shower, and headed to Franklin where I met Paul Milius at a restaurant called Stoney River. Paul said he'd been there hundreds of times, knew the owner, and could get us a private room where we wouldn't be bothered by anyone.

After we took our seats and ordered something to drink, I looked at Paul and said, "What did you think?"

"What you did to Lana made me wonder what Frye will do to me tomorrow," he said.

"Testifying in a murder case isn't for the faint of heart," I said. "Do you think you're up to it?"

"Is it really necessary at this point?" Paul said. "If you take Lana out of the mix, and I think you did that pretty well, they still don't have motive. They haven't proved I killed her, and they haven't offered anything in the way of motive."

"Maybe not, but you have to admit it's a pretty strong circumstantial case. They have testimony that Kasey threw the tea in your face, they have the hotel security videos and your driver that put you at the scene at or near the time of her death—not to mention your own admission to the police—plus they've proven you slapped her and they have the DNA match. It's pretty strong, Paul. I've seen juries convict on less."

"So you're saying I should testify?"

"I don't really know. Juries like to hear defendants deny committing the crime, especially if the denial is convincing or sincere or emotional. But they also *expect* defendants to deny committing the crime, so to be honest, I don't know how important it really is for you to get up there and say, 'No, I didn't kill her.' It will give Frye another chance to stand there and say, 'Okay, you admit you were having an argument with her but you didn't kill her. You admit you went to her room but you didn't kill her. You admit you slapped her but you didn't kill her. How convenient for you. And oh, by the way, what did she say that made you slap her?'"

"And I'll have to answer?"

"Probably not. It isn't a dying declaration and I can't think of any other exception to the hearsay rule, so it's hearsay and I can object and the judge will probably tell you not to answer. But every single member of the jury is going to want to know the answer to the same question, and if you get up on the stand and weasel out of having to answer it, they're not going to like you very much. Have you decided what you're going to say if you end up having to answer that question under oath?"

"She insulted my mother."

"Kasey? Kasey insulted your mother? That's why you slapped her?"

"Yeah."

"We'll talk about it some more in the morning," I said, "but for now, let's just go with the idea that you're not going to testify."

Paul and I stayed at the restaurant for about an hour, and after that, I drove out to Charlie's house and had a couple beers with her and Jack. It was nice. We sat on her front porch and smelled country smells and listened to music and drank the beers and forgot about Paul and Lana Milius for almost three hours. I drove back to the house on Belle Meade around ten o'clock, watched television for about an hour, and fell fast asleep in the recliner in the den. About three in the morning, I must have heard something unusual because my eyes flew wide open and I sat straight up in the chair.

Sitting on the couch, right across the room, was a man. He was pointing a pistol at my chest. I cursed myself underneath my breath for not taking Tilly's warning more seriously and slowly leaned back in the recliner.

"Are you Lana's guy?" I said as calmly as I could.

"I guess you could say that," he said.

"You here to kill me?"

"Depends. I thought we might talk a little first."

CHAPTER 42

"Would you state your name, please?" I said as I opened my defense of Paul Milius with the one and only witness I would call.

"John Smith."

"Where do you live, Mr. Smith?"

"Right now I'm living here in Nashville, on Second Avenue, but I'll be leaving soon."

The man on the witness stand was the same man who had been sitting in the den of my rented home the previous night pointing a pistol at my chest. He was handsome and leathery, mid-thirties, probably five feet, ten inches tall and a hundred and seventy pounds. His hair was short and chestnut brown, his face covered with a thick mat of short stubble. He'd come to court wearing navy blue pants and a white, button-down shirt with a striped tie. No jacket.

"Mr. Smith, we might as well get right to the point. Do you have direct knowledge of who killed Kasey Cartwright on the morning of December eleventh last year?"

"I do."

"Tell us what you know, please."

"I killed her."

Judge Graves's gavel slammed so hard I thought he'd broken it as the crowd behind me erupted again.

"Get up here, right now," he demanded, and Pennington Frye and I walked to the bench.

"Just what do you think you're doing, Mr. Dillard?" the judge said.

"Putting on my defense. It's going to be a pretty good one."

"This is just like yesterday," the judge said. "You can't just…you can't just come in here and do whatever you like!"

"I'm not doing anything wrong, Judge. Nothing improper. This man came to the house I was staying in at three in the morning. Just last night. If you'll let him testify, I think you'll be interested in what he has to say, although I'll tell you right now his testimony directly refutes everything Lana Raines-Milius said yesterday."

"I kicked her out of the courtroom."

"And you can kick this guy out, too, if you think he's lying or if it gets too strange, but you can't pick and choose the witnesses, Judge. This case is what it is. You let Lana up there. You have to let Mr. Smith testify. Fair is fair. Give Mr. Frye the same amount of room you gave me on cross-examination. Let him try to tear the guy apart. I won't say a word."

"This whole thing stinks to high heaven," the judge said. "Step back."

I walked back to the lectern and started right back in.

"You said your name is John Smith, correct?"

"That's right."

"And you said a minute ago that you killed Kasey Cartwright?"

"I did."

"Where did you kill her?"

"In room 3100 at the Plaza Hotel here in Nashville."

"When did you kill her?"

"It was back in December. The night of the tenth and eleventh."

"What time did you kill her?"

"Around two thirty in the morning."

"How did you kill her?"

"I strangled her with my hands."

"And finally, why did you kill her?"

"I was paid to kill her and Mr. Milius, but Mr. Milius left the room before I could get to him."

"Who paid you?"

"Lana Raines-Milius."

"She paid you directly?"

"She wired the money to an offshore account that I control."

"How much did she pay you?"

"The contract price was $5 million for both of them, but I only received half of that amount on the front end. There's a bit of a disagreement going on right now between us over whether I should be paid the rest of the money."

"Can you describe in detail for the jury how you came to be hired and how you went about killing Miss Cartwright?"

"I was initially approached by an associate who is located in London. He had been contacted by someone else who had been contacted by someone else who had been contacted by someone else. I don't even know all the contacts myself or exactly how the job originated. I don't want to know. It's an extremely secretive, complicated process. But eventually, the offer made its way to me and I accepted it. I gathered a small team and we came to Nashville. One of my men contacted Mrs. Milius initially and provided her with a specially programmed cellular phone. She gave the phone to Mr. Milius's personal assistant, a man named Alex Pappas. Mr. Pappas then provided us with information on the targets, the date, where the job was supposed to take place, all of those things. He also used money he received from Mrs. Milius to wire half the contract price to an offshore account. We started the reconnaissance process, figured out how best to get myself into the hotel room, and procured some equipment. Then on the night the job was supposed to be completed, I entered the hotel through the service entrance dressed as an employee, went to the thirty-first floor, and used a microcontroller to read the key code and unlock the door. The room was a suite, and I waited in the bedroom closet for the targets to come in. My plan was to wait until they were in bed and then shoot both of them in the head, but I started to think something had gone wrong when the girl came in alone."

"What time did she come in?" I asked.

"It was around one forty-five. She just sat down on the couch out in the den of the suite and started watching television. I stayed in the closet and waited. Around two twenty or so, I heard a knock on the door, the television went off, and then I heard a man talking to her. Their voices got louder—they were arguing—and then all of a sudden I heard a smack. The girl ran through the bedroom into the bathroom and slammed the door. The man came in and was saying, "Kasey, I'm so sorry. I'm so sorry. Open the door." I couldn't go after him while she was in the bathroom because I didn't know whether she'd taken her phone in there with her and might be calling the police. She screamed at him to get out and the next thing I knew he said, "Okay, I'm going," and he was out the door and gone. She came out just a couple minutes later, and I immediately did what I'd come there to do. I didn't shoot her, though. She was so small I just grabbed her by the throat and it was over in just a minute."

"So you only completed half the job."

"That's right."

"Why didn't you finish it later?"

"I intended to, but in the immediate aftermath of the girl being found, there was a lot of attention being focused on Mr. Milius, so I decided to back off and wait. I left Nashville and then just a couple weeks later one of my associates received word that Mr. Milius had been arrested for the murder and that they no longer wanted us to complete the job."

"Aren't you afraid that by coming here and offering this testimony you'll be arrested for murder, Mr. Smith?"

"Not really."

"Why not?"

"It doesn't matter if they arrest me. They won't be able to keep me."

"You'll escape?"

"Yes."

"And you'd be willing to kill anyone who got in your way?"

"Absolutely."

"Would you mind telling the jury a bit about your background?"

"I was a United States Navy Seal assigned to the Joint Special Operations Command for almost ten years. I killed seventy-eight people during that time using a sniper rifle and participated in dozens of raids against suspected terrorist targets. Four years ago, I was seriously wounded during an operation in Yemen. It took me a year to recover. When I was ready to come back, I was told I was no longer welcome. Too old, they said. Unreliable because of the time I had to take off. Behind on the training and the tactics and the missions. They pretty much tossed me aside. I wasn't ready to quit, so I made myself available to an organization that had been doing contract killings all over the world for decades. I did several jobs for them and then decided to just go it alone."

"So killing is your business."

"Killing is my business."

"And Kasey Cartwright was just a target to you?"

"That's all any of the people I've killed have been. Just targets."

"Why are you here, Mr. Smith? Why are you risking arrest and incarceration and possibly the death penalty to testify in this case?"

"I may be a killer," he said, "but Lana Milius is far worse than me. I just wanted everyone to know that."

"So why don't you just kill her?" I asked. "Why don't you use your resources and stalk her and gather your intelligence and plan it out and kill her and get away with it?"

He smiled and leaned forward into the microphone.

"Believe me, I've thought about it," he said. "But this is a lot more fun."

CHAPTER 43

I had to hand it to Pennington Frye.

I'd done the same thing to him that he'd done to me the previous day. I'd surprised him with a witness and delivered an incredibly strong blow to his case. But rather than give up and ask meaningless questions or stand in front of the witness and just repeat his testimony—which so many bad lawyers do—Frye tried to turn it.

He hadn't said a word during my direct examination of John Smith—not one single objection. When I was done, after Smith had delivered what I thought had to be the death knell: "Believe me, I've thought about it. But this is a lot more fun," Frye stood up, walked to the lectern, leaned back a little, and took a long, slow deep breath. He raised his chin, squared his shoulders, and clapped.

"That was some performance," Frye said.

"Thank you," Smith said with a smirk. I wished immediately he hadn't said it.

"May I see some identification?" Frye said.

Smith said, "Sure, no problem," reached into his back pocket, and produced a driver's license that was eventually passed to me. It identified him as John Smith, address 5617 Second Avenue, Nashville, Tennessee 37208. It looked legitimate to me, and Frye didn't say anything to the judge or anyone else about it. He just asked the bailiff to hand it back to Smith.

"Is John Smith your real name?" Frye said.

"It is."

"Don't you think John Doe would have been more appropriate?"

"My name isn't John Doe."

"It isn't John Smith, either, is it, Mister whatever your name is?"

"I just showed you my identification," Smith said.

"What you just showed me is fake. When did you decide you needed to testify in this trial, Mr. Smith?" Frye asked.

"Yesterday. As soon as I heard about Lana's testimony. I flew in from Montana. Got here just after midnight and paid a visit to Mr. Dillard."

"So you, the self-described international assassin, the freelance James Bond, have been following this trial closely?"

"I've been fascinated," Smith said. "It's been good theater. And besides, Mrs. Milius still owes me two and a half million dollars, so that's kept me interested."

"You didn't happen to bring along any documentation of this $2.5 million wire transfer you spoke of earlier, did you?"

"I sure didn't."

"Do you plan to collect while you're here?"

"I haven't decided yet."

"And you don't have any proof of your presence in Kasey Cartwright's hotel room that night, do you?"

"The proof of my presence is that she's dead."

"How much did Mr. Milius pay you, Mr. Smith?"

"I beg your pardon?"

"How much did he pay you to take part in this charade? What's it worth to risk arrest and trial for murder these days? Ten million? Twenty?"

"He didn't pay me—"

"Are you a trained actor, Mr. Smith, or does lying just come to you naturally? Because this just doesn't make any sense to me. There isn't one bit of evidence that you were anywhere near Kasey Cartwright's room that night. All we have is you coming in here right at the end of the trial and saying, 'I did it.' Did you really think you can fool a jury—a group of twelve intelligent people—with a stunt like this?"

"I don't really care what they believe," Smith said, "but I'm telling the truth."

"If you don't really care what they think, then why are you here? No, no, never mind, don't answer that. You're here to indulge your sense of justice and fair play, correct?"

"Something like that."

"The international assassin, the man who says he's killed almost a hundred terrorists, the military hero, the man who says killing is his business, has a strong sense of justice and fair play. Is that what you're telling us?"

"I'm telling you I killed the girl."

"Of course you did," Frye said. "So I suppose we'll just arrest you and let Mr. Milius go with our deepest apologies, and then we'll put you on trial with absolutely no evidence except your last-minute confession—oh wait, we won't put you on trial because you're a trained international assassin and you'll escape. So I suppose I should just ask the court to dismiss the charge against Mr. Milius and everyone should just go home?"

"You could arrest Lana Milius if it would make you feel better, but I won't be around to testify."

"Thank you, thank you for the sage advice, Mister whatever your name is. How much did you say Mr. Milius paid you to come in here and tell this tall tale? It really is Paul Bunyanesque."

"Mr. Milius didn't pay me anything. His wife paid me."

"I've already grown tired of listening to your lies," Frye said. "Your presence here disgusts me. Will you kill me for saying that?"

"Not unless somebody pays me."

"Maybe Mr. Milius will give you a little bonus. You're excused."

CHAPTER 44

Frye delivered his closing argument, I delivered mine, and the judge read the jury instructions before lunch. I'd left the courthouse immediately and spent the day with Jack and Charlie. I checked in with one of the bailiffs I'd befriended during the trial around two thirty and he told me he'd heard a lot of arguing and even some cursing going on in the jury room. At five fifteen, my cell phone rang. It was the judge's clerk.

"They have a verdict."

We got through the rush-hour traffic as quickly as we could and arrived at the courthouse just after five thirty. Everyone took their places in the courtroom, and the judge called the jury in. A man named Ted Hanson, fifty-two years old, had obviously been elected foreman because he was carrying the verdict form in his hand.

Judge Graves waited until the jury was in the box and seated before saying to Paul, "Mr. Milius, please stand." I stood with him.

"Ladies and gentlemen of the jury, have you elected a foreperson?" the judge said.

Most of them nodded.

"Will he or she please stand?"

Ted Hanson stood.

"Mr. Foreman," the judge said, "has the jury reached a unanimous verdict?"

"We have, Your Honor," Hanson said.

"In the case of *State of Tennessee versus Paul Milius*, how does the jury find?"

"We find the defendant guilty."

CHAPTER 45

I tossed my suitcase into the trunk of Caroline's car and climbed into the passenger seat. I was so relieved to see her. I knew she'd been suffering because of the new medication. Her cheeks were hollow, she'd lost more weight, and she'd told me she was sleeping between twelve and fifteen hours a day. My sister, Sarah, had been spending a lot of time with her along with Lilly, but I was glad to be home. She was my wife. Taking care of her when she was sick was my job.

It was just after nine o'clock on the day following Paul Milius's conviction. Caroline was picking me up at the airport. I'd taken a commercial flight from Nashville because Paul Milius had fired me as soon as we walked out of the courtroom. I'd said, "I'm sorry, Paul," and he'd responded with, "You're damned right you are. You're the sorriest lawyer I've ever run across in my life. You're fired. I hope I never see your face again."

"I heard on the news that Kasey Cartwright's grandparents filed a $100 million wrongful death suit against Paul Milius first thing this morning," Caroline said as she started the engine and pulled out of the parking space.

"Not surprised," I said.

"I'll bet you're exhausted."

"It was a pretty wild ride. Oh, I talked to Lilly last night. She said she let Randy move back in."

"Yeah, I think she's forgiven him for straying, or thinking about straying. It was hard on both of them. It's been hard on everyone."

"How long was he out? Six weeks?"

"Seven weeks and two days. Lilly counted. Did you get a chance to have breakfast with the juror?"

"I did," I said. "His name was Hanson. He was the foreman. He was a good guy, very complimentary."

"Complimentary? Toward you?"

"Yeah."

"Then why did they convict your client?"

"He said it went back and forth several times, that it got pretty heated in the jury room. But in the end, they took all the theatrics out. They decided to ignore Lana's testimony completely and ignore John Smith's testimony completely. That left them with Paul being in Kasey's room near the time of death. It left them with the argument earlier at the CMT show and the tea being thrown into Paul's face and Paul admittedly slapping her in her room and the DNA evidence. He said it was enough and he was comfortable with it. He also said they would have liked to have heard Paul deny it himself."

"Why didn't he take the stand?"

"He was terrified that he'd have to answer *the question.*"

"Ah," Caroline said, nodding her head. We'd talked about the mysterious question a few times before. "I wonder what she said to him that made him slap her."

"I think I know," I said.

"Really? How?"

"Smith, or whatever the hell his name is. He told me what she said the night he showed up at the place I was staying. He said he was in the closet when they were arguing. Paul came into the room and immediately started trying to get Kasey in the sack. He was saying things like, 'I miss you so much, baby,' and 'I need you so bad.' And you know what she says to him? She says, 'Cameron Jones's dick makes yours look like a tooth-pick.' And he slapped her. The man was so egotistical that he wouldn't take the witness stand because he was afraid the jury would hear that Kasey had insulted the size of his manhood. I don't know if it really made that much difference because I don't think the jury would have liked him, but his ego wouldn't even let him take the chance."

"So Lana wins," Caroline said.

"I guess so. Her young rival is dead and her adulterous husband is in prison. His company will soon be on the auction block, and it wouldn't surprise me to see her end up with it. And I'm sure she'll wind up with the estate and everything that goes along with it."

"What will happen to Paul?"

"He'll get fifteen years and he'll probably serve close to ten, but they'll send him to a minimum security camp. It won't be a picnic, but it won't be hell on earth, either."

"Will he appeal?"

"I'm sure he will, but it won't get reversed."

"You don't think he did it, do you?"

"Nah. Smith killed her."

"Life can be so unfair sometimes," Caroline said.

I reached over and patted her hand, thinking about the cancerous tumors that had wrapped themselves around her bones.

"It sure can, baby," I said. "It sure can."

EPILOGUE

John Smith, whose real name was Michael Baker and who hailed from Bozeman, Montana, sat with his back against a tree and gazed down at the house a couple hundred yards away. It was always lit, although this late at night, most of the lights were off. An easy breeze rustled through the newly bloomed leaves above him; the night was cool but pleasant. Smith took his cell phone out of his pocket, pushed a few buttons, and heard the whir of the blades as they began to spin.

Smith had spent many hours in the woods on the Xanadu estate since the trial had ended in Paul Milius's conviction for second-degree murder. Normally, he would simply have disappeared and gone about his business, but he couldn't get past the feeling that he'd been defeated, and that he'd been cheated in the process, and John Smith, formerly known as Mike Baker, didn't like to lose and he damned sure didn't suffer cheaters. So he had decided to stay a while longer. He'd contacted some associates and requested some equipment. It had arrived almost immediately.

Smith had watched the house and the grounds during the morning, during the evening, and at night, getting the routines down, trying to find the rhythm of the

people and the place. It didn't take him long at all to figure out that late at night would be the best time. She'd
be drunk. She would have taken an Ambien, and all the
servants would have gone home. Lana's personal assistant
had quit and she hadn't hired another. Paul was in prison.
Nobody but Lana lived at Xanadu.

But this night was a special night, the one he'd been
waiting for. It was Saturday and the lawyer was there.
Finally, the lawyer was there. He'd arrived almost two
hours ago. He and Lana had been served drinks in the
atrium, dinner in the dining room, then more drinks in
the atrium. Smith even knew what they'd eaten: poached
lobster and beef filets, grilled asparagus, roasted potatoes,
chocolate mousse. The drone had hovered just outside the
atrium windows, then the dining room windows, silently
displaying everything on Smith's cell phone screen while
the servants served and the masters gorged themselves.
The resolution on the cameras was amazing.

Now the servants had left and Lana and the lawyer
had moved to the bedroom. As soon as Smith realized
they were heading upstairs, he'd flown the drone back to
his little hideout, quickly outfitted it with some special
equipment, and now it was on its way back to the house.
Smith flew it to the southern wing, second floor, to the
first of six leaf-shaped windows that surrounded Lana's
bedroom—the bedroom that overlooked the Olympic-
sized indoor-outdoor pool and the most luxurious patio
Smith had ever seen.

Attached to the bottom frame of the six-bladed hover
drone, just beneath one of three cameras, was a cocked,
double-action Smith & Wesson .357-magnum pistol,

and inside the chamber of the pistol was a specially-constructed cartridge (built very much like an armor-piercing shell) that would reduce Lana's overpriced, luxury, leaf-shaped window to powder. Molded around the upper frame of the drone was roughly one thousand grams—about two pounds—of C-4 plastic explosive.

Smith watched the monitor on his phone as the window came into view. When the drone was about fifty feet away, he pushed the button that fired the pistol. The window disintegrated in an explosion of glass. Smith maneuvered the drone through the opening and into the bedroom. He could see Carl Browning scrambling off the side of the bed, naked. He pushed the button that would detonate the C-4 and looked up.

Fire and glass erupted from the bedroom as the explosion roared and the earth seemed to vibrate. Then all was suddenly quiet as smoke rolled lazily from the openings that had recently contained windows. Smith watched silently for a minute or so as Xanadu bled. He wondered what Lana Raines and Carl Browning had thought when they looked up and saw the drone float into the bedroom.

As he started down the hill away from the house, Smith took one last look down at his phone and smiled to himself.

Like the house behind him and the lives of the people he'd just killed, the screen was empty.

Thank you for reading, and I sincerely hope you enjoyed *A Crime of Passion*. As an independently published author, I rely on you, the reader, to spread the word. So if you enjoyed the book, please tell your friends and family, and if it isn't too much trouble, I would appreciate a brief review on Amazon. Thanks again. My best to you and yours.

Scott

ABOUT THE AUTHOR

Scott Pratt was born in South Haven, Michigan, and moved to Tennessee when he was thirteen years old. He is a veteran of the United States Air Force and holds a Bachelor of Arts degree in English from East Tennessee State University and a Doctor of Jurisprudence from the University of Tennessee College of Law. He lives in Northeast Tennessee with his wife, their dogs, and a parrot named JoJo.

ALSO BY SCOTT PRATT

An Innocent Client (Joe Dillard #1)
In Good Faith (Joe Dillard #2)
Injustice for All (Joe Dillard #3)
Reasonable Fear (Joe Dillard #4)
Conflict of Interest (Joe Dillard #5)
Blood Money (Joe Dillard #6)
River on Fire

Children's Stories
An Elephant's Standing in There
A Ride on a Cloud

52653732R00165

Made in the USA
San Bernardino, CA
27 August 2017